DEAD IN THE WATER

Hailey Edwards

Copyright Information

Edited by Sasha Knight

Copy edited by Kimberly Cannon

Cover by Damonza

Interior format by The Killion Group

Gemini, Book One

Camille Ellis is the Earthen Conclave's golden girl. Her peculiar talent solves cases with a single touch, and she isn't afraid to get her hands dirty. But the brightest stars cast the deepest shadows, and her grim secrets lurk just beneath the skin.

A routine job goes sideways when the victim's brother barges into the investigation demanding answers. Consumed with grief, the warg will go to any lengths to avenge his sister's death. Even if it means ensuring Cam's cooperation at the jaws of his wolf.

CHAPTER ONE

Seven out-of-state crime scenes in seven months was seven too many. Every fourth Wednesday dread ballooned in my chest during the short drive from home to the local marshal's office until I marveled that my ribs didn't crack under the pressure. On those days I had fallen into the habit of perching on the edge of my task chair, fingers cramped from gripping the desk's edge as I stared at the phone, willing it not to ring.

But it always did.

Each time I hung up with Magistrate Vause, every time I agreed to consult on a drowning case, I told myself *this* was the last one, that I had atoned, that Lori wouldn't want me to keep punishing myself. Then I grabbed the go bag I kept packed by the door and drove to the airport.

Today's call came as prompt as all the others, and so here I was, in a new state, at a fresh scene, decked out in my investigative best. Pressed slacks. Button-up blouse. Light jacket enchanted with a chill spell against the Deep South humidity that breathed steam down my neck the second I stepped from my frosty rental car onto the shade-dappled asphalt.

"You must be Agent Ellis." A wiry man made thinner by his sweat-drenched dress shirt approached me with his arm extended. His sleeves were rolled up past his forearms, and mud stained the cuffs. "I'm Decker Comeaux, and this is my crime scene. I appreciate you flying out to consult."

Out being Villanow, Georgia.

"No problem." I clasped hands with him. The low hum of his magic made my fingertips tingle. "Elf?" His grip went limp. "You're using a third-tier glamour." A quality one at that. "Those ears must be hard to cover."

The fingers of his opposite hand smoothed over the rounded top of one ear as if searching for a point. He dropped his hands and shoved them into his pockets to give them somewhere to go. Or maybe just to keep them away from me. "They warned me you had unusual talents."

I massaged the base of my neck, fingers slipping down into my shirt collar like a warning label was a physical tag I could hide. "Unusual is one word for it."

Plenty of fae were unique. I wasn't special. Just different.

His smile conveyed the exact right amount of empathy. It made me wonder if he practiced the expression in a mirror before work each day. "The body is this way if you'd like to take a look."

Like wasn't the word I would have used. I wasn't in Villanow because I wanted to be. I was here because the method of death called to me, a perverse obsession I had as much control over as taking my next breath.

Comeaux eyed me expectantly, and I realized I hadn't answered him yet. "Sure." I tossed him the key fob to my rental. "Do me a favor and hold on to that."

After tucking the hunk of plastic into his pocket with an amused twitch of his lips, he led me past eight unmarked black SUVs overflowing the cramped parking area at the trailhead. We hiked for a while until a crater emerged from among the trees. It must have spanned three miles across. A more generous soul might have called it a dead lake, but that sounded morbid given the circumstances. Morbid or not, the empty bed was as dry as the grass crunching under my feet. Thanks to the summer draught, only the deepest portion of the bowl retained any water.

Sweat trickled down my nape despite the cool weight of my jacket. Water, no matter how fresh, always carried the underlying scents of decomposition. Rotting fish corpses. Molding leaves. Urine. Feces. Ponds were swimming pools for bacteria, and my sinuses burned when I caught that first whiff of decay, stinging my nasal passages like I had inhaled a gallon of saltwater.

Seagulls cried.

Waves crashed.

Lori gurgled as her head vanished beneath the swell of white foam.

"Are you all right?" He squinted in the same direction as me. "That's where she was found, if that's what you're wondering."

"Yeah." Throat tight, I ripped my gaze from the water. "I figured."

"We documented the scene then moved the remains to a tent." He indicated a white geodesic affair sheltered by the limbs of forgiving pine trees. "There's a fan hooked up to make the heat more bearable, but the smell…"

Nothing anyone could do about that.

Showing the pond my back made the skin covering my spine twitch. But now that my sights were locked on the dingy material pitched several yards away, I focused there and on what waited inside for me. No. Not what. *Who.*

My fingers didn't shake when I lifted the tent flap. If they had, I was ready to blame all the chai I had tossed back during the long drive from the airport out to the middle of nowhere. Three other fae were congregated inside, and the tight-knit group had parked themselves in the far corner where a steady *click, click, click* made it obvious they were here for the cooler air and not for the body.

They were all men, so it must have taken balls to stand beside a dead girl and whine about a few sweat stains under your pits.

A ripple effect hit as each head turned until I held the group's collective attention. What they saw on my face sent them bolting out the rear flap and left me alone in the oppressive heat with the victim. Drawing out the moment, I examined every sweltering inch of the interior except for what lay before me, until I caught myself reading the ingredients off a label of hand sanitizer and forced my gaze front and center.

A neon-blue tarp stretched across a commandeered picnic table. I got downwind of the oscillating fan, and it blasted me full-on with the stench of meat gone ripe from too much sun. A white and wrinkly maggot inched over the emaciated curve of the victim's hip, and some primal response had me tasting what I ate for breakfast in the back of my throat. I kept down the cereal bar, but it was a near thing, and I didn't think I would ever taste strawberries again without remembering this moment.

A young girl was curled on her side on top of the plastic. She was nude, and her pale skin held a blueish tint. Without touching her it was hard to tell if temperature was a factor or if the reflection of the tarp was playing tricks on me. Her fragile limbs had bloated from her time spent in the water, and the flesh had burst in places like overstuffed sausage casing. One arm stopped at the elbow and exposed bone protruded, white and gleaming. Chestnut hair clung like freshwater seaweed to her spine, dripping brown-tinted liquid that flowed in rivulets off the table to quench the thirsty earth below.

A quick check over my shoulder confirmed I was still alone. With the sun at his back, Comeaux's silhouette was visible through the thin fabric separating us. He was half-turned, arguing with someone. One of the guys I had spooked away from the fan was probably tattling on me.

"Enough with the stalling," I muttered. Skin crawling with grim resolve, I pressed a single finger to the girl's spine through the filter of her damp hair. Residual power answered that barest touch with sickening force, and I had my answer.

Godsdamn it. I recognized the magical signature. She was one of ours all right. Another victim of a serial killer agents of the Earthen Conclave had nicknamed Charybdis, after a mythical sea monster.

The girl's species eluded me. A hint of earthy magic convinced me her people were native to this realm and not a descendant of Faerie. Indigenous magic registered on my scale in an indeterminate way, making the brush of Charybdis's power all the easier to identify for it.

The gallon jug of hand sanitizer I had been eyeballing sat on the ground near the exit flap. I walked over and pumped until clear goo dripped through my fingers then massaged out the worst of the echoes before resuming my visual examination.

Milky-blue eyes gazed at the stump of her missing arm. Her thin lips mashed together as though even in death she held back a scream. The roundness of her childish features churned a memory that frothed with kinship for the dead. I stared at her hard, willing a resemblance to another lost girl to surface, but there was none. Whoever she had been, she was no Lori.

The quality of light changed, and I assumed Comeaux had joined me. "Has her family been notified?"

A rusty growl vibrated on the air. "Her family found her."

Startled, I lifted my head.

A tall man filled every inch of the entryway. Wiry muscle packed his lean frame. Dark hair was slicked to his scalp. Grungy stubble covered his face. Feral intelligence sharpened his hazel eyes as they pierced mine. Bands of black ink circled his wrists, and towering cypress trees grew from them to trace up his forearms. A small figure flashed on the inside of one wrist when he shoved aside the tent flap, but he lowered his arm before I could identify the marking. Mud covered his naked torso. His jeans were soaked through and held low on his hips by determination alone. His feet were bare and caked with dirt. Haggard and exhausted, he looked like a man primed to walk off a cliff's edge just to get life the hell over with so he could finally get some sleep.

"Agent Ellis—" Comeaux shouldered into the tent, giving the man a wide berth, "—this is Cord Graeson. He's the victim's brother."

Gravel churned in Graeson's voice. "Her name was Marie."

Marie Graeson. One more name etched onto my private wall of remembrance. "I'm sorry for your loss."

Comeaux allowed a moment of silence to lapse before prompting me. "Well?"

My gaze skated from Comeaux back to Graeson. I had a hard time not looking at him while he was staring a hole through my left ear. "Should Mr. Graeson be present for this?"

The grizzled man stalked toward me. Hostility wafted from his skin like pungent cologne. "*Mr.* Graeson will be part of this investigation until the sick bastard responsible for Marie's death is brought to justice."

The primal region of my brain quaked in its boots, but I kept my voice steady. "She's one of mine," I confirmed. "Her injuries mirror those of the previous victims."

The marshal scratched his chin. "Can you tell what type of fae did this?"

"No," I lied as cold sweat popped down my spine. "I'm sorry."

Graeson's nostrils flared—scenting my fib?—and my hands became of sudden interest to him. Damn it. He must smell the hand sanitizer. Our gazes locked, and his irises gleamed with a golden sheen. He knew I had touched her even if he hadn't figured out why.

"It was worth a shot." Comeaux rocked back on his heels. "Do you want to visit the site?"

About as much as I wanted Graeson to punch me in the face with those cinder blocks he called hands. The knuckles bending his weathered fingers were scarred and thick like a pro boxer's would be.

"Sure." I sidestepped Graeson's intensity, exited the tent and waited for Comeaux to join me. "Lead the way."

The banks surrounding Pilcher's Pond sloped in a gentle downward curve past the edge of the trail Comeaux and I had taken to reach the tent. The ground was bare and cracked, the weeds dead and brittle underfoot. He veered to the left and began sidling down the incline toward the basin. I stepped where he did and focused on keeping my feet under me. After a few minutes, curiosity forced the question on my mind past my lips. "What's the deal with Graeson?"

"He's beta to the Georgia alpha, a guy named Bessemer." Comeaux kept his voice pitched low. "If Graeson wants to investigate his sister's death, it's within his rights under the Native Species of Magical Origins Act. We aren't required to share our information with him, but we can't refuse to answer his questions either." At my incredulous look, he shrugged. "To them, this is pack business. The murder took place on Chandler pack lands. They take care of their own."

Beta. Pack. Alpha. One plus one plus one equaled a potentially serious four-legged problem.

Cord Graeson was a warg, a dominant one to hold the position of second-in-command to a man like Bessemer. And he knew I had lied to him. That decision would bite me on the ass sooner or later, maybe even in the literal sense.

Mindful of the debris one would expect to find in sediment—Christmas trees, license plates, beer cans, fishing line—we picked our way toward the mile-wide stretch of gray-green water cupped in the remaining depression.

As I studied what remained of the pond, faint ripples arrowed from its center outward. Something was down there, and it was headed our way. Fast. A sharp twist in my gut had me tasting strawberries for the second time that morning, but Comeaux swatted a fly, and I forced my jaw to unclench.

The cloudy depths parted over a young woman's cotton-candy-pink head, and my lips opened with surprise. Shocking indigo eyes framed by black lashes beaded with moisture studied me. A purple neoprene suit hugged her body and accentuated her slight curves. The outfit belonged on a diver, but I didn't spot a scrap of equipment on her. No mask, no regulator, no tank. Nothing to indicate what the hell she was doing bobbing like a cork in the middle of a crime scene when she looked like she ought to be planning a homecoming dance or rallying votes for class president.

"Find anything?" Comeaux called to her.

"A barrette." She held a blue plastic bar molded with bows aloft for our inspection. "Hardly worth getting my hair wet."

Forget her hair. The girl had been swimming bare-faced in the same stagnant water as the corpse. I wanted to shower and scrub my skin pink just thinking about it. "How can you tell it belonged to the victim?"

"She was wearing the matching clip when her body was fished out of the pond this morning." She snapped the closure shut. "I assisted."

Well okay then.

The girl sliced her willowy arms through the water. As she swam closer, I noticed robin's-egg-blue nail polish flashed on her fingertips. When only a swath of muck separated us, she spun around, winked at me over her shoulder and began hauling herself out of the water backward by walking on her palms.

"Do you need…?" I strangled on the word *help*.

Gradient scales in sunset hues covered her from the pronounced dimples bracketing her spine down as far as I could see. Sunlight glinted off each scalloped disc, and I squinched my eyes but couldn't look away. "You're a mermaid."

"Are you a detective? If not, then you should be." She settled three feet in front of me and twisted so her tail bent where knees would be on a human. Pink fins the same shade as her hair curled around her. "Your powers of observation *astound*."

Unlike the men in the tent, my patented glare didn't faze her. Otherwise her tail would have seared like a pan-fried salmon fillet.

"Harlow is a commercial diver. She's our inland waterways consultant," Comeaux offered. "She's on loan from St. Augustine."

A mermaid living on a peninsula. Color me surprised.

Comeaux coughed into his fist. He might have been laughing. I wasn't sure which one of us was the butt of his joke. Then I realized I had spoken out loud. *Fudge.* So much for interdepartmental cooperation.

The girl scraped dirt from under her nails. "Where are you from?"

"Three Way—"

Laughter burst from her tiny bird's chest. "Is that on a map or a life choice?"

"—Tennessee," I ended flatly.

She sat there, gazing up at me, eyes sparkling. Maybe she expected me to bristle. But the Three Way jokes had gotten old thirty seconds after I signed the lease on my slot in the Three Ways from Sunday RV park. So, yes. Three Way, Tennessee. Home of people cursed to insta-judgment and pervy stares for sharing their home address with strangers.

"Can you email me scans of what you have so far?" I asked Comeaux, electing to ignore Flipper. "When you get the autopsy report, I'll need a copy of that for my records too."

"Already working on it." The elf pulled a phone from his pocket. "All I need is the address where you want it sent."

I passed Comeaux one of my business cards and tapped the fine print. "Use that one."

The elf punched the address into his contacts with his thumbs faster than I could have with all ten fingers. "Done." He pocketed the card. "The results will take a few days."

"Not a problem." Buzzing at my hip made my heart skip. I excused myself and turned my back to reinforce the illusion of privacy. "Ellis."

"Check your email," Magistrate Vause ordered in lieu of a greeting. "A marshal outpost in Wink, Texas has reported the discovery of an apparent drowning victim matching our killer's M.O."

"That's not possible." The scents of water and decomposition swamped me, and the back of my throat began to tickle. "It's been less than twenty-four hours since his last victim was identified." *His* victim, because the magic signature vibrated with distinctly male undertones. "Charybdis is precise. He's not going to deviate now. There are also geographical considerations."

The pattern of his attacks was moving in a clockwise motion through southern states. Texas was a stretch.

"That is your opinion, and it will remain speculation until you verify or invalidate this latest incident."

I smoothed the curve of an eyebrow with my pointer finger, mentally bracing to see another waterlogged corpse so soon. "Give me ten minutes."

"I'll be expecting your report on the Villanow incident." She ended the call with a decisive click.

Another state. Another body. Eight victims. Were we still talking about one killer? Some fae hunted in packs. That might explain the range. No. The magical signatures were identical. No two creatures gave me the same buzz. Not even relatives. Not even twins. I could always tell when Lori…

Cool winds.

Damp sand.

Delicate footprints erased by the slap of angry waves.

"Catch me if you can, Cam."

Grief ricocheted through my chest, the razor edge of loss so sharp my heartstrings felt severed anew. The crushing weight of the memory bowed my shoulders and bent my knees. I began power walking toward my rental car before realizing I hadn't said my goodbyes. I had left the sorry excuse for a pond behind without a second thought.

Shoving a hand in the pocket of my wilted slacks, I groped around and came up empty. *Comeaux*. I had given him the keys so that when—*if*—a panic attack struck, I couldn't run from the scene before my job was done. Not without asking for the fob back and humiliating myself.

Pounding footsteps sent relief fluttering through me. I wouldn't have to endure a walk of shame today after all. Comeaux reached me at the same time as I arrived at my ride.

"That's it?" He mopped the sweat beading on his forehead with a fast food napkin from his pocket. "You're leaving?"

"Another body has been found." Another drowning victim, another small punishment to chip away at what remained of my sanity. Accepting Vause's commission to work these cases had been a mistake, but sign up I had and soldier on I would. "You have my contact information if you think of anything else."

"Was it worth it?" He crumpled the damp paper. "Did you get what you needed?"

Latent power buzzed in my fingertips at the thought of the corpse. "I got what I came for."

Confirmation Charybdis had claimed another victim.

I held out my hand. "Key, please."

He slapped the fob across my palm. A sweaty business card curled around it. His.

"I'll be in touch." He leaned against a nearby tree and took relief in its dense shade. "Safe travels."

"Tell Flipper I said bye." I slid behind the wheel of the sedan while Comeaux hooted. I dropped the chunky fob into a cup holder then pushed the start button and pulled onto the road.

Wink, Texas, here I come.

CHAPTER TWO

The Wink Sinks of Winkler County were two sinkholes barely visible from the highway. I knew, because twenty-four hours after leaving Villanow, I sat in the teensy Chevy Spark I picked up at the Midland International Air and Space Port while squinting in what the GPS assured me was their general direction. Even though from this distance there appeared to be more fence posts spearing the cracked earth than water filling the basins.

Motion on the horizon snagged my attention, and what I thought at first was a heat mirage solidified into a feminine outline. She strode across the scrubland toward me with a bounce in her step, and I couldn't peg her affiliation based on her attire. Short shorts. Cropped T-shirt. Cowgirl boots. Civilian or off-duty marshal?

I slid my palms over the leather-bound wheel and gave serious thought to turning around and driving right back to Midland. From there I could hop a plane to Memphis. Drive the couple hours' home. Sleep in my own bed while the old guilt nibbled at my conscience one bite at the time.

Knuckles rapped on glass, and I jumped as a grinning face haloed by wavy pink hair peered in at me. Recognition sparked, and I jabbed the button until my window lowered. "What are you doing here?"

"You're not the only consultant working overtime on Charybdis." Flipper braided the ends of her hair, the gesture so automatic as to be a habit. "Nice toy car, by the way."

Ignoring the jab at my subcompact ride, I leaned out the window and stared down at her legs bared by the teeny scrap of lavender denim masquerading as shorts. *Legs*. On a mermaid. Sure, there were ways for merfolk to walk among humans, but none of them were legal because each of them required ritual sacrifice.

I pointed at her scuffed teal cowboy boots. "Where did those come from?"

"An outlet mall off I-20." She pivoted her heel, admiring her foot. "I can give you directions if you like."

"Cute," I said dryly.

She buffed her chipping nails on her shirt. "That's what they tell me." When I reached through the window to nudge her away from the door, she danced out of reach and pointed at my hand. "Hey. No touching."

Interesting. Flipper had herself a secret. Two of them I bet. Both crammed into her outlet mall cowboy boots.

I tucked my hand back inside the vehicle. "Were you sent to fetch me?"

"Nope. I was walking to my car to grab a bottle of water. It's hotter than a firecracker lit on both ends out here." She scuffed her heels on the pavement, and her impish face screwed up into a mask of innocence. "I saw you sitting here and decided to come ask if you were waiting on an engraved invitation or what."

I snorted. Hard. It was as close to a laugh as I had gotten in too long. The alien noise rang out in the confines of the car. Flipper peered through her lashes, sporting a pleased grin, like I was a nut she had finally cracked. Or like maybe she thought I was cracked period.

She had no idea.

"Here." I passed her one of the two chilled bottles of water I had purchased at the gas station ten miles back. "It's yours if you want it." I wasn't sure I could bring myself to drink them without a few squirts of a liquid flavor enhancer, and the store hadn't carried any of the familiar tiny squeeze bottles.

She hesitated with her arm half-extended, and I remembered. *No touching.* Careful of the sloped metal, I balanced the bottle on the roof of the car. Flipper waited until my window whirred up and glass stood between us before she cranked up her swagger, sashayed over and accepted the offer.

"Much appreciated." The interior muffled her voice.

It was as close to a thanks as I expected.

Never thank the fae. We see it as an admission of a debt owed, and most of us collect favors like teens collect selfie apps.

The seal cracked, and Flipper drank the water down until she sucked air. I tucked the remaining bottle into my jacket with the hope the same spell that kept me from sweating through the fabric would keep it cool too. Heat rippled over my skin, the sun promising to burn, when I joined her on the cracked blacktop. The car locked with a chirp, and I angled my chin toward the site. "Should we…?"

"Yes, you should." She walked backward in the opposite direction. "I still have to grab a few things."

"Hey. Do me a favor?" I didn't wait for a nod before tossing my key fob to her. "Keep that safe for me."

"Uh, sure." The oblong chunk of plastic vanished into one of her micro pockets. "I can do that. I guess."

"I appreciate it."

The first responders, probably local marshals, had opened the gate surrounding Wink Sink No. 1 through magical means. I still smelled the burning metal. Faded signs posted in the surrounding area warned of "Unstable Ground". Most were sun-bleached, and graffiti artists were treating them as blank canvases. One particularly artistic soul had used a permanent marker and drawn fanged mermaids copulating.

I wondered how Harlow felt about that, and then wondered if she had been the one who drew them.

I could have ducked through one of the holes snipped through the chain link—probably by local teens using the sinks as a make-out spot—and saved myself a dozen footsteps. But the severe woman guarding the entrance was watching me through the nictitating membranes covering her vivid jade eyes, so I stuck to the beaten path.

"Can I help you?" A purr rumbled through her words.

"I'm Agent Ellis. Magistrate Vause sent me to examine the body."

Her chest continued to pump with throaty noises. "Got any ID on you?"

"Sure." A six-pointed star pinned to an ID wallet bearing the Earthen Conclave's seal weighted down the breast pocket of my jacket. I flashed it for her. "I won't take up much of your time."

One touch, and I would have all the confirmation I needed to file my report and go home, see my family and refill the well before plunging back into the depraved underbelly of faekind. Leaving Aunt Dot to her own devices for long stretches of time was almost as bad of an idea as being here was in the first place.

"Okay." Her rough pink tongue swiped over her chapped bottom lip. "I still can't grant you access until I clear it with my supervisor."

"She's with me," a familiar voice boasted from a safe distance away.

The rasp of the woman's mocking laughter made me wish Flipper hadn't vouched for me. I don't think it did either of us any favors. When Flipper angled to walk past and the marshal blocked her, I knew that it hadn't.

Red slashed Flipper's cheekbones. "Find another mouse to play with."

"Go filet yourself." She bared needlelike teeth and hissed. "I don't take orders from sushi."

Water splashed onto the ground. The fresh plastic bottle in Flipper's hand crinkled in protest as liquid flowed over her knuckles. The promise of violence flavored the air, and the fingernail on my right hand's middle finger loosened with a dull throb. The keratin spur hidden in a sheath of skin in my nailbed was itching to extend, prick the kitty's paw and absorb a dollop of magic through her blood. I pressed my thumb over the tip of my middle finger to hold the nail in place.

"Tell me we don't have a problem here," a whiskey-rich voice drawled. "Tell me I'm wrong and that a cat fight wasn't about to break out at my crime scene." The newcomer glanced back at the sink, and his gaze went distant. "There's a dead child a half dozen yards away." His focus shifted back to us. "Show some respect, or get your asses back in your cars and leave."

The cat woman's throat fluttered in response, but she didn't speak a word. He accepted her brand of apology then studied me with a critical eye. I returned the favor, absorbing his copper eyes and the mahogany curls flattened by sweat.

"I'm Camille Ellis." I didn't offer him my hand, didn't want to draw concern for my wobbly nail. "Magistrate Vause sent me."

"Vause, huh?" His full lips slanted down at the corners. "Somehow I doubt picking fights with my team is what she had in mind." He touched the woman's arm, and her purr ramped up a few decibels. "Go relieve Rebec. Tell him he's got the gate."

As she sashayed away, she aimed a final smirk over her shoulder at Flipper.

To my surprise, I found the bipedal mermaid positioned at my side, standing an arm's length away with her feet braced apart. "Your marshal is the one with an attitude problem. Not Agent Ellis."

My jaw scraped the ground. Flipper was standing up for me?

"I'm aware of the issue." He pointed to me and then to her. "Don't put me in the position of having to choose consultants over a fellow marshal again, or you're both gone."

Ultimatum issued, he returned to the sink.

We were left behind, dismissed. All the better for me to get in and get out faster. The fewer questions asked of me, the better. "You didn't have to do that."

"Bullies can only retain their power through our silence." The lilting way spoke made me think she was quoting someone or that she said it often.

I stared after the curly-haired marshal. I couldn't help it. The man was gorgeous, and the way he moved had to be illegal in some states. His predatory gait reminded me of Graeson before I banished all thoughts of the snarly warg. "Is he the man in charge?"

"Yes, indeed. Jackson Shaw." Flipper wrinkled her pert nose. "Be careful around him."

The name sounded familiar. I must have heard it recently. Or maybe I'd read it on the briefing.

"He's an incubus," she informed me. "Mermaids have immunity thanks to our cousins, the sirens, but you need to stay on your toes. I'll thump you in the ear if you start stripping or ask him to sign your boobs instead of your report."

I glanced down at my creased black dress pants and rumpled polka dot blouse. With my ash-blonde hair twisted out of my face and my storm-cloud-gray eyes bruised from lack of sleep, I wasn't in any danger of being crowned Miss Texas. But my pride stung nonetheless. The guy was an incubus, and the cat woman had given me a more thorough going-over than he had.

“Thanks.” Even after I said it, I was pretty sure I didn’t mean it.

CHAPTER THREE

No tent meant no private access to the body. I found the victim resting on a dull brown tarp spread over the parched ground. A second layer of plastic covered the girl from the chin down, preserving her modesty and giving her the illusion of a child napping. Two grim-faced marshals guarded the remains. One swept her piercing emerald gaze back and forth across the fissures spreading for hundreds of feet in all directions. The other had placed himself between the body and the eerily blue water.

I leapt a fissure the width of my hips to reach them. "I'm Camille Ellis." I tucked flyaway hairs behind my ears. "I'm here to examine the body."

The woman casting stink-eye at the cracks spared me a glance. "I've been expecting you."

That didn't sound ominous at all.

She ignored me after that, so I got to work and knelt beside the corpse. From a distance, I hadn't noticed the dark hair covering the head was only a finger's length or that an Adam's apple disturbed the line of the throat. The usual routine of searching the deceased's face for hints of Lori screeched to a halt. "This victim is male."

He had died trapped in that androgynous state some boys transition through on their way to manhood.

"We noticed," the woman said.

I lifted the plastic and choked before what I was seeing fully registered. Hand covering my mouth, I flung myself away from the corpse. I braced on my palms and knees with my head hung over a deep crevice and filled it with the turkey club I'd eaten for lunch. From the waist up, the boy resembled any of the other victims. Besides the obvious difference. From the hips down, his bones had been picked clean of meat.

No wonder the marshals were on high alert. A predator hunted those waters. Charybdis? I doubted it. He was too fastidious. The compressed timeline bothered me too. Not to mention the victim was the wrong sex, and mutilation on this scale wasn't his style. He collected arms—one limb per victim, to be precise—not legs. And he drowned his girls first. This boy… Gods, I hoped he hadn't been alive when the creature who killed him began eating.

"Here." A bottle of water appeared in front of me. "Rinse out your mouth with this."

I stuck out my hand, and the Good Samaritan slapped the drink across my palm. When I stopped tasting bile, I lifted my head high enough to see Flipper standing barefoot across the fissure from me. She had stripped out of her boots and cutoffs. The purple neoprene top was back on, but she wore a lime-green bikini bottom instead of the metallic tail from yesterday. I craned my neck but didn't spot any fins or gills.

"What are you about to do?" I wiped my wrist across my mouth.

Her toes flexed in the loose sand, and her orange-and-blue toenails sparkled. "I need to interview the locals."

A red mask hung from her fingertips, which answered my next question. "You're going in the water."

She raised a candy-colored eyebrow. "Unless you're volunteering…?"

A shudder rippled through me hard enough to squeeze my empty gut again. "No."

Flipper twirled the rubber strap around her pointer and started walking toward the waiting marshals. "In that case, I left your fob in my right boot in case I don't make it back."

"Hey," I called after her. "Be careful."

Her answering smile dazzled. "You too."

It was on the tip of my tongue to ask why I had to be careful. Unless whatever living in Wink Sink No. 2 sprouted legs, I was safe here on the high ground. Right?

"You consulted on the other cases." The marshal from earlier offered me a rune-covered hand, and I let her haul me to my feet.

"Yes." Magic blasted through that contact, and I jerked from her grasp. "You're a legacy." I rubbed my palm. "A powerful one."

She was also a half-blood, but I didn't say so. Most didn't appreciate the reminder they were half-human.

"A legacy?" She tugged her long black hair up into a ponytail. "I've been called a lot of things, but never that. What does it mean?"

"Your mother or father was born in Faerie." That explained her strength. "The closer the tie to Faerie, the stronger the magic." She rubbed the markings covering the fingertips of her left hand together. "I hope I didn't say anything wrong." The urge to explain myself to her surprised me. "My gift is like a stream of consciousness. Classifications pop into my head and then they fall out of my mouth."

"That's a cool talent." For the first time since meeting her, the marshal locked gazes with me. Her eyes were bright and as sharp as a knife's blade. "I'm Thierry Thackeray."

The name rang a distant bell, but as with Shaw, my brutal travel schedule meant my brain was too stuffed with the names and faces of colleagues for me to skim any details off the top.

She indicated the tarp. "Are you finished with the body?"

"No." A bitter taste lingered in my mouth. "I need to—" I swallowed. "The condition surprised me. The others were…not like that."

"I won't tell you it gets easier." She patted my shoulder, and raw power zinged down my arm. "It doesn't, but you do find better ways of coping. My favorite is finding the person responsible and—" as though poised to say one thing, she instead said another, "—I make them pay."

Despite the heat, a biting chill crept over my skin. I believed her.

Someone called her name, and Thierry excused herself. I breathed easier with her out of touching distance. Suddenly I sympathized with Flipper and her hands-off policy.

I was returning to the body when the ground trembled. I caught myself before turning my ankle in one of the smaller cracks, and pressed a hand to my stomach. Everyone on site had gone still. "You felt that too, right?" I asked the remaining marshal.

He held a finger to his lips. "Shh."

I shushed.

The quaking began again, harder this time. Splashing broke the silence. I turned my head slowly and spotted Flipper struggling against a thick blackish-purple band encircling her waist. She leaned back in the water, arms slicing in a backstroke that got her nowhere. She kicked her legs—where was her tail?—but she didn't budge.

"She's in trouble," I realized. Then louder, I said, "*She's in trouble.*"

The marshal finally pried his gaze from the sink to glare at me. "In about thirty seconds, if she doesn't get her shit together, we're all going to be in trouble."

"What are you talking about?" I flung my arm toward Flipper. "She can't help us if she can't help herself."

A high-pitched shriek gurgled, churning bubbles that frothed the water and obscured Flipper's torso. No one budged to offer her a hand. Good thing I had two spare ones.

I jumped across a craggy fissure and landed in a wobbly crouch three feet from the water. My ankles quivered, knees locked. Flipper was close, but the edge of the water was closer. The rippling surface mocked me as though the sink were laughing at my cowardice.

Salt burned my eyes, turned my skin sticky. I ran faster than the gulls flew. "Momma," I screamed over and over until my lips moved in a silent plea for help come too late.

I banished the memories cramping my muscles. I had no time for the paralyzing grief. I should wade into the sink. Hell, I should use one of the ruptured pipes sticking out of the dirt at its edges as a springboard and dive in after her. I should, but I *couldn't*. I squatted there, useless and shivering while the earth rumbled and Flipper's pink crown vanished.

"Ellis," Thierry shouted. "Get out of there."

I held my ground. Easy to do with terror seizing my limbs. "Not without her."

The marshal landed in a tense crouch beside me. "She's a mermaid. You know how sturdy those are, right?"

Except Flipper was different. Mermaids didn't exchange tails for legs when it suited them. Mermaids didn't tuck their hands under their armpits to avoid touching a person who could classify them. There was more to her than bright hair and skimpy clothes.

The kid had a secret, a big one if she was willing to take it to her grave, and it was going to get her killed in front of a live audience unless I rallied help.

Each gasp rang across the baked earth, every frantic splash echoed through the silence. Without gills or an oxygen tank, she would drown. I once stood paralyzed on a white-sand beach as a life snuffed out instead of wading in and braving the unknown. Fear be damned, I would never stand by again.

"She's just a kid." No one with so much life ahead of them should be robbed of living every moment of it.

As a mermaid, Flipper was in her element as far as the others were concerned. But at this rate her element was going to snap her spine like a twig, assuming it didn't drown her first.

"I don't know if I have enough juice for this." Thierry stood and shook out her arms, and the left one lit up with green light that shone from her runes. "Go stand with the others. I need room to work."

"I can help." I fanned the fingers of my right hand, and this time I let the rush of adrenaline nudge my fingernail until it flaked off and the hollow spur curved over my fingertip. I extended my hand toward her. "I'll need a drop of blood."

Fingers curling into her palm, she stared at her runes, and their light reflected in her eyes. Blood was a powerful weapon that could fuel harmful spells that targeted the donor. All those grim possibilities washed over her face, but her composure broke when Flipper screamed, and she set her jaw. "Don't make me regret this."

Thierry gripped my hand and hauled me onto my feet. "Little pinch," I warned her as the spur pierced the back of her hand. A drop of blood welled before she healed the wound. Her magic crushed me under a wave that sent me crashing to my knees. Searing pain marked my left hand, and phantom runes danced over my skin.

"Freaking monkeys," she muttered. "Shaw? Little help here."

The skin covering my arm stung and tightened. I wasn't strong enough to act as a conduit for so much power. It was cooking me from the inside. I had to force it out again before it burnt me to a crisp. Instinct guided me to extend my arm toward Flipper. Energy burst from my palm, shimmering across the choppy expanse and leaving steam in its wake. It pierced the surface of the water with a hiss. Flipper cried out as the pulse swept through her. Limbs twitching, her head fell limp on her shoulders.

The thing holding her gargled a furious roar.

Thierry grasped my wrist and slammed my palm into the dirt. "Do that again, and you'll kill her."

I nodded to show I understood since my mouth wasn't working yet, and let the remaining power leach into the soil.

Another shriek made me wince as an eggplant-colored appendage burst from the water. Hundreds of feet long, it whipped through the air and slammed against the cracked earth. The ground buckled under my knees. Fist-sized suction cups speckled the underside of its slimy flesh, but there was nothing for them to grip but loose dirt. The thing couldn't haul itself out to escape the magically electrified water. Seeming to realize that a heartbeat later, it dove, yanking Flipper under with it.

My nails raked over the crumbling soil. *"No."*

"We should have nipped this in the bud years ago," I heard Thierry say to someone.

"Thierry, no." The rumble of Shaw's voice was unmistakable.

"We can't leave it here," she argued. "More people will die, and I don't want those deaths on my conscience."

"It's too dangerous," he growled. "We need to regroup and call for backup."

"There's no time." Her tone rang with finality.

He sighed the words "Be careful" and didn't try to change her mind again.

Thierry breezed past me and dove into the water. Butterfly strokes carried her toward the center of the sink where she vanished beneath the frothing waves.

A fierce growl poured over my shoulder. A glance back at the incubus dried the spit in my mouth. His skin had gone pale. His fingers elongated into claws that curved with killing edges. The warmth in his copper eyes had faded to a desolate white, and the soulless weight of his gaze made me believe if my actions had just gotten Thierry killed, I had signed my own death warrant.

A full minute lapsed. Shaw exhaled the seconds under his breath.

Eight tentacles as thick around as my torso exploded from the water. The one cinched around Flipper's midsection was the dark band I'd noticed earlier, and she hung limp in its grip. Thierry dangled from another, spluttering for air. The others hammered the ground, creating new fissures. Limbs swept out, knocking marshals onto their asses and pounding the dried earth to dust.

I ducked as one of the foul-smelling arms whistled over my head. I whirled to check on Shaw and found him sawing through the flesh with his razor-sharp claws. Ichor wept from the wound, but the creature didn't give up, and neither did the pissed-off incubus.

The threat to their own roused the other marshals into action. The uninjured ones rallied around Shaw. He abandoned the severed tentacle and took a running leap that ended in a splash. He swam for Thierry and began climbing the arm shaking her like dice in a dealer's cup, as if whatever was down there wanted to get its Yahtzee on.

I remained crouched in a rigid pose while the team sprang into motion, cutting at tentacles or restraining them while someone else slashed at them. The need to help them beat in my chest, pinched at my temples, but the old fear hit me harder. My eyelids dropped shut, and a cold sweat bathed me.

Warm sand squished between my toes. A sharp pain radiated up my leg, and I plopped down to pick a thin piece of shell from my heel. Fat tears welled as I stared at my crimson-stained fingers. A taunting voice rang over the dunes. I shoved to my feet and limped after a darting shadow. The full moon was our only light. Daddy said it was made of cheese, that the dark spots were holes chewed by space mice. Momma said space mice had eaten his brain.

"Crybaby. Crybaby," the breathless shadow sing-songed as she barreled into the surf. "Cam is a crybaby."

Teasing laughter once muted by the crashing waves dissolved into screams.

A stampeding hippo slammed into me and knocked me flying. When I remembered how to breathe again, I sucked down hungry gulps of air. Dirt coated the back of my throat, making me cough as I rolled onto my side. Okay, so maybe it hadn't been a hippo, but those tentacles were all muscle, and I might as well have been a fly and it the swatter.

I shoved upright and absorbed the chaos surrounding me. Had I really thought this crime scene couldn't get any worse? Black goo squished through my fingers when I braced in a puddle of congealing blood to get back on my feet. Its magic radiated up my arm. *A kraken?* In a sinkhole in Nowhere, Texas? Really? Its faint energy tinkled over my skin, and I knew what I had to do.

Of the eight original tentacles, three remained. Two hung suspended over the water. The one squeezing Flipper and the one constricting Thierry. The way Shaw was climbing the latter meant it wouldn't last much longer. I had to move fast. The third remaining arm swung in wide arcs before slapping the ground then sweeping left to right as it bowled over the marshals in pursuit. My best hope was reaching that one, but I had to hurry. A guy wielding a flaming sword was in hot pursuit of it. No pun intended.

I chased after the swordsman, slipping in muck and stumbling over uneven earth. When I reached him, I yelled, "Don't sever it." His glare called me a crazy woman. I didn't argue, but I did tack on, "*Yet.*"

He hesitated, and that was opening enough for me. "Help me pin it down."

Three other marshals rushed the thrashing tentacle, throwing their combined weight on top of it until their dogpile held it immobilized. I rushed over, crossed the fingers on my left hand for luck, then pricked the rubbery hide with my right. My wrists slapped together and stuck from fingertips to elbows, forming a solid limb. Pain blossomed down my arms, through my shoulders, and the pale flesh purpled like bruising.

Magic burned white-hot as it burrowed under my skin, suffusing the muscles with strength to wield my new appendage. My heels clicked together, bound with unseen ropes. From ankles to armpits I formed a solid trunk. My toes stung as the nails elongated, piercing the ends of my boots and plunging deep into the brittle ground to steady me. Soon I commanded a scaled-down replica of the kraken's tentacle, and I had to pray I was close enough to do some good. I was rooted to the spot. This one-woman rescue mission wasn't going anywhere.

"Okay." I struggled against the onset of panic over my limited mobility. "I got this."

Fudge. Fudge. Fudge. I don't have this. I never should have shifted to this degree.

The more of my body I altered, the faster I burned through the magic filtered from the source. I didn't have long before I was drained, and two shifts in one day left my conjoined knees quivering.

"Hold the arm for as long as you can," I ordered the stunned marshals. "I might need to use it again."

The slack-jawed group gaped up at me, and one adjusted her weight like she was thinking of jumping me next. It was cat woman. *Nice.* I didn't wait for her to make her move. I unfurled my new appendage, reached across the water and grasped Thierry's leg. Shaw read my intent, nodded once, and severed the limb at his eye level. The sudden drop made me gasp as the muscles in my arm and back strained. One of my toes ripped from its anchor in the ground as I struggled to counterbalance Thierry's weight. I bent like a tree being uprooted, but then her feet touched the sandy shallows, and the strain vanished.

"Shaw." Safe on the shore, she picked off suckers that left red welts behind. "Get out of there."

Nodding, he released the oozing stump and hit the water with a splash. He didn't resurface. Thierry took a full step forward, her light's reflection emerald and lethal, but then his head breached the surface, and she hauled him out to stand beside her.

With Shaw out of the way, I cast my arm toward the kraken one last time and lassoed Flipper around the hips. A bestial roar rattled my teeth as the nubs from its severed limbs writhed. The marshals restraining the landlocked appendage shouted as the kraken's thrashing bucked them. Rescuing Flipper became a tug-of-war with the submerged beast I couldn't win without ripping her in half.

Limbs quivering from exertion, I cried out, helpless as the heady dose of power taken from the kraken expired. Stinging magic marched over my body, hungry ants nipping at tender skin. Flesh paled. Bones and muscles slid into their natural shape. Ragged toenails shrank to their normal length. The bindings on my arms and legs loosened, and I slipped free of them. Feet numb and tingling, I limped to Thierry. "What's Plan B?"

"The same as Plan A." Thierry wiped black fluid from around her eyes. "We get her out of there. I can handle the rest." She twisted her limp ponytail into a tight bun. "We don't have much time. As soon as the kraken shakes off the marshals pinning its arm, it's going to dive. If it goes down, we won't get Harlow back. No one in their right mind would follow that thing into the sink, and that includes you, even if I have to sit on you to stop you from trying."

Me? Follow the creature into its home turf? Into the *water*? My spine turned to jelly at the thought, which would make it hella difficult to swim, because the mind-numbing truth was, I might. I had fought too hard to save Harlow to give up on her now.

Shaw craned his neck. "Rodriguez, get over here."

"On it, boss." He was the sword-wielding fae. His scowl bounced between Thierry and Shaw. "If I drop my sword, I want solemn vows you'll help me retrieve her when this is over."

Shaw nodded. "Done."

"Sucker," Thierry sang under her breath.

He popped her on the ass, and she growled. That move had sexual harassment lawsuit written *all* over it.

While they engaged in a battle of silent wills, Rodriguez waded knee-deep into the sink. With reverence, he sheathed his blade in a scabbard running parallel to his spine then swam toward Flipper. Reaching behind himself, he drew his sword, and it blazed with flames the sink failed to extinguish. Even treading water, it didn't take him long to hack through the muscular tissue holding her aloft. Hauling Flipper back to shore winded him more than the short battle. Safe on dry land, he dropped to his knees and spread Flipper on her back. He shot me a thumbs-up, which I took to mean she was still breathing.

"Guess it's my turn." Thierry set off at a jog toward the final tentacle. "Climb off it, guys." She made a *hurry up* gesture. "Stand back or you'll get fried too."

The marshals rolled aside and ran a safe distance away long before Thierry's left hand made contact.

Green light exploded from Thierry's palm, and the creature's death scream rattled my eardrums. Its thrashing intensified, and its remaining limb swiped at her, but she hung on and ramped up the light show. The blackish skin peeled where she touched it, flaking off and fluttering on the hot breeze. Joints ripped like torn seams, revealing orange flesh with black veins. The creature gurgled once more then fell silent except for the hissing of seared meat. Thierry wobbled where she stood, but Shaw was there to catch her when she collapsed.

I had to move my tongue around to find enough moisture to swallow. I stared at my hand, flexed my fingers and wondered what the hell I had been thinking borrowing an unknown source of magic from a legacy. Thierry had peeled that creature like the skin off a grape. It was a miracle acting as her conduit, even for those few seconds, hadn't fried me.

Whistling brought my attention back to Rodriguez. His shirt was fisted in his hand, and he walked away, cleaning his blade with the damp fabric while baby-talking to his sword. Flipper remained motionless on the ground. Another fae—a medic I hoped—leaned over her. She had thumbed Flipper's eyes open and pressed a palm to the girl's frail chest. Out of energy, I dragged one foot after the other until I reached her side and collapsed to my knees. Her arm extended toward me, fingers lax. My hand hovered an inch above hers, so close I felt the damp coolness of her skin, but I recoiled.

Comforting or not, Flipper wouldn't thank me if she woke and discovered that I had touched her and learned her secrets.

"Is she breathing?" I asked the medic, who nodded in the affirmative. "Okay, Flipper, so you're not dead. That's good. Not dead we can work with." Giddy, I sank back on my heels. This was why I had become a marshal, why I had accepted the Earthen Conclave commission. I wanted to prevent grim-faced marshals from knocking on doors in the wee hours of the morning carrying a burden that would crush the recipient of their news. So often, as with Charybdis, I failed. But not today. Today I had made a difference. "Can you open your eyes? Something?"

"Harlow."

I frowned. "What?"

"My name—" her words slurred, "—is not Flipper."

I wiped a trickle of warm crimson from under my nose. I tasted copper sliding down the back of my throat as I rubbed my face clean on the tail of my shirt. Staggering to my feet, I held still until the ground stopped bucking and jumping underfoot, then scowled at the kraken. It was still dead. I had just expended too much energy then stood too quickly.

"Be right back," I promised.

Finding the young boy's body again was tough. Mostly because not much was left of the victim after the kraken finished pulverizing the area. It didn't take a lot for me to read magic on remains. I touched a shattered elbow and felt…nothing. No residual magic from Charybdis. No inborn magic from the boy. He was a blank slate.

This victim had been human, his only crime stumbling into an area populated by lethal fae that few mortals knew existed in order to avoid them. His parents would never know the truth of how his brief life ended. I sank to the ground and sat there beside him so he wouldn't be alone. Even though he was past caring about such things, I wasn't, and I hoped I never would be.

CHAPTER FOUR

I crashed hard after the incident at the Wink Sinks. That much I remembered. The conclave comped my room in a budget motel on the fringes of town so I could recuperate. I remembered that too. But I woke stiff from my earlier exertions and with the nagging sense of having forgotten something. Expending as much magic as I had without warming up first came at a cost, and I got the feeling from the dried crust around my mouth that I had just paid the bill.

A dark outline leaned over me, and I jerked upright so fast I almost cracked my forehead against Harlow's before she leapt backward. After a moment's heart-stopping pause, I swallowed my panic and slumped back against my pillow. "What the hell?"

"I was worried about you." She scraped polish off her fingernails. "You've been drooling on that pillow for thirty-six hours. It's almost midnight."

"What?" I blinked my eyes clear of their hazy film. "That's not possible."

Aunt Dot would have a heart attack if I didn't check in soon. She had expected me home the day after my impromptu trip to Wink, and since she was my next-door neighbor, she had probably been sitting in her bathrobe on the front porch staring down the dirt road leading into town, waiting on my pickup to round the bend until well past her bedtime.

Calling her at this hour was out of the question. She hated email and thought cell phones were brain cancer waiting to happen. My cousin Isaac, her youngest son by five minutes, lived beside her. I would text him to explain the situation as soon as Harlow left, and he could pass on the information when he met his mom for breakfast the next morning. It was too little, too late, and yes, somewhat cowardly, but it was the best I could do at this point.

Once the gong in my skull stopped ringing, I squinted up at Harlow. Curls spilled over her shoulder, and the light fixture cast a golden halo around her head like an angel fallen from Candy Land. "How did you get in here?"

"I bribed the overnight manager." She rolled a thin shoulder that caused her yellow mesh top to slide down her arm, revealing a black bra strap. "He was cheap, and it was worth it." A heavy pause. "I owe you one."

"No." Debts made me uncomfortable. "You really don't."

"Why did you do it?" The question came out stilted. Maybe she wasn't sure she wanted the answer.

"You had my car key." I worked up the energy to smile. "What else was I supposed to do?"

She braced her forearm on the mattress beside me in a dent that made me wonder if she hadn't been sitting just so for a long time before I woke. "I told you where I left the fob."

I wrinkled my nose. "You thought I was going to stick my hand down the boot of a kid I barely know?"

"I'm not a kid." She toyed with the ends of my hair, using her thumb to scratch off mud flakes that drifted onto the sheets. "I'm sixteen."

Sixteen. Had I ever been that young? Four years separated our ages, but Harlow's wardrobe pushed the envelope of decency and her personality sparkled. My pantsuits and frown lines left me dull by comparison. "Is it rude of me to ask—?"

"What's a nice mer like me doing in a place like this?" She cracked a smile. "I'm on the mermaid equivalent of Rumspringa. I get a year to walk on land before I decide if I want to hang up my fins and embrace life on two legs for good."

"I didn't realize that was an option." The tradition wasn't one I had ever heard of before.

Pursing her lips, she mashed a mud flake into dust against my mattress with her thumb. She shook her head once, seeming to decide against whatever she might have confided. Her next words closed the topic of mer traditions and started a new one. "I meant what I said earlier. You risked your life for me."

"A lot of people did." The teen scoffed, but I insisted, "It was a team effort."

"They would have let me die," she said matter-of-factly. "I messed up. Big time."

I didn't disagree on either point. "Why is that?"

"I'm not what I pretend to be." She flicked a piece of dirt off her nail, and her tone sharpened. "But you already knew that, didn't you?"

I pushed upright, wincing as my temples throbbed from the sudden motion. Either that or the persistent, gnawing hunger raking claws across my abdomen. "I didn't touch you."

Relief flickered across her features. "Then please don't." She scraped her even front teeth over her bottom lip. "If you saw inside me, you wouldn't like what you found half as much."

"I doubt that." The vote of confidence made her twitchy, so I shifted gears. With thirty-six hours' worth of sleep purring in my tank, I was itching for news. "You look good. Their medic does excellent work." I didn't see a mark on her. "How did everyone else fare?"

"Seven injured at the scene." Her voice came out tinny. "One fatality."

The urge to rest my hand on hers and offer comfort twitched in my fingers, but I honored her wishes. "Is Thierry okay?" The last time I saw her, Shaw had been carrying her toward a truck.

"She's fine."

"I'm glad to hear it." That meant I wouldn't have dreams of incubus assassins dancing through my head tonight. "She's the one who did all the heavy lifting."

"That's not how I remember it." Harlow ducked her head and pressed her index finger to my wrist. No. I got no buzz off her skin, no feedback from her magic. She was touching something *on* my wrist. "Thanks, Cam. I mean it. For having my back."

Cam. No one had called me that in years. In that moment I realized how much I had missed the intimacy of it.

I studied her, curious why she would grant me a boon and even curiouser about the warm weight pressing against my pulse. I raised my arm. A simple bracelet strung with luminous peach-toned pearls hung from my wrist. Intricate designs were carved into the surface of each one. How had I missed it? Had we bumped heads that hard? "What's this?"

"I dive for raw materials." She worried one of the holes in her top with her index finger. "I make things sometimes."

I ran my finger over the bumpy grooves. "You made this?"

Another shrug.

"It's beautiful."

Harlow scooted her chair back and stood. "You should eat something. I can hear your stomach growling from here. Menus are there, and my number's on the pad by the phone if you want some company." She pointed at a dusty frame housing a bland flower mural on the wall beside the door. "I'm right across the hall. If you need anything, holler."

I was pawing through the top drawer of my nightstand before she reached the door, and mulling over my options before she shut it behind her.

Raised voices greeted me when I emerged from the shower. It was late, a shade past midnight, and I had missed the cutoff for room service. If I wanted to eat before climbing back into bed, I was going to have to brave the diner across the street. Wrapped in a threadbare robe embroidered with the hotel's insignia, I towel-dried my hair, twisted it up on top of my head, then followed the yelling to my door where I peered through the fisheye lens into the hall.

Harlow stood with her back pressed against the door to her room and her hand circling the knob. Thierry stood on her left side and Shaw on her right. His shadow engulfed her, and it gave that side of her face a bruised appearance. Three other people crowded the hall between our rooms. Their backs faced me. Two women and a man. At the point of their triad, a brunette with tangled hair yanked into a lopsided ponytail shook her fist while screaming at Harlow. An older woman with a long, gray braid stood behind her to the left while the brown-haired man supported her elbow.

Before I could rein in the impulse, I had taken the knob in hand and twisted until the latch gave and a crack appeared in the door. They didn't hear the rattle or click over the shouting. They didn't notice the gap either. Their gazes were fixed to the left. I knelt and stuck my eye to the hairline space.

"...is dead because of you..."

"...knew what he was getting into..."

"...kids grow up without their father..."

A pang rocked me when I realized they were talking about the marshal who had died in the line of duty. Why or how the woman had fixated on Harlow puzzled me. Part of me worried it was my fault. If Harlow hadn't stayed behind an extra night in Wink to babysit me, she would have left town before the widow got a chance to confront her. The whole situation made me that much more nervous about the secrets she was keeping.

"I'll take this up with the magistrates," the angry woman cried. "*She* never should have been on the scene."

"She's a consultant." Thierry sounded short on patience. "The Southeastern Conclave assigned her to help us with a difficult case."

"She's an abomination," the woman shrilled.

Emerald light blossomed in Thierry's palm. The brunette didn't appear to notice, as she was locked in a glaring contest with her, but the older woman did, and she took a shuffling step back, dragging the man with her.

"The conclave doesn't discriminate." Thierry ground the words out through a clenched jaw. "I'm sorry your husband lost his life. Jasper was a good man, but you can't hold Ms. Bevans responsible."

Discriminate? Against mermaids? Or against Harlow in particular? I zeroed in on the leggy girl inspecting the faux woodgrain on the door with a quiver in her lip. What did these people know that I didn't? How much had I missed while I was recuperating?

The grieving widow lunged at Harlow, fingers curved into ragged talons, but smashed against Shaw's chest when he stepped in front to shield her. "You heard what my partner said." He gripped the woman by her shoulders. "This is over, Mrs. Rebec. If you have a problem with the consultants hired by the conclave, then make good on your threat. Take it up with the magistrates."

"Letitia," the brown-haired man said. "This won't bring Jasper back. Come on. Let's get Mom home. I'll call the marshal's office in the morning and lodge an official complaint."

The old woman wrapped an arm around her daughter, and Letitia allowed her mother to lead her away.

"You okay?" Thierry planted her hands on her hips and grimaced in Harlow's direction. "We got here as fast as we could."

"I've had worse." Wincing, she brought her fingers up to probe her jaw. "That woman has a killer right hook."

"You can press charges," Shaw offered. "She jumped you in the hotel lobby. That's assault. The night manager is willing to give a statement that he pulled her off you. We can also get our hands on a recording of his phone call to the marshal's office as evidence."

When he shifted to stand beside Thierry, the light moved with him, and I swallowed a gasp. Harlow's delicate jaw was split and bloody. The widow must have been wearing her engagement ring when she socked her. A bare hand wouldn't have caused that kind of damage.

"No." The maybe-mermaid ducked into her room. "I don't want to hang around. I've already stayed longer than I should have."

"I'll be right back." Thierry excused herself and crossed to my room before knocking gently on the door. A satchel weighted down one of her shoulders, and she shoved it behind her. "Anyone home in there?"

I would have heard the smile in her voice even if I wasn't staring right at it, which made it easier to brush off my knees—and my dignity—and stand. When I opened the door, so much blood rushed into my cheeks I felt lightheaded. "I heard shouting."

"There was a misunderstanding." Thierry skimmed my appearance, and her grin widened. Flushed, I yanked on my towel turban and let the damp waves of dark blonde hair fall over my shoulders. I doubted it was much of an improvement, but it made me feel less frazzled by comparison. Her gaze slid past my shoulder to where I had laid a pair of brown slacks and a lavender blouse at the foot of the bed. "It's settled now."

As confident as she sounded, I hoped she was right and the woman wouldn't make a second attempt before Harlow left. Some fae took the whole eye-for-an-eye thing literally.

"You look like you're getting ready to go somewhere." She pulled a phone from her pocket and checked the time. "Did you book a red-eye or something?"

“No.” I hadn’t cracked open my laptop long enough to plan that far ahead. “I crashed pretty hard. I’m starving, and room service hours ended around ten.”

“There’s a coffee shop across the street.” Her shoulder bumped the door. “It’s crap, but it’s close. Join me for a cup?”

The way she said it made me think I didn’t have much choice. Good thing my stomach wasn’t about to argue.

CHAPTER FIVE

Much to my dismay, the shop across the street turned out to be cramped and gloomy, and the air inside smelled the way I imagined soup would if it were made of sweat socks left to boil on the stove overnight. The booths were upholstered in cracked vinyl with pocked yellow foam rupturing from the seams. The stink of ancient cigarette smoke puffed out when my weight hit the cushion, and the sharp edges raked at my pants like tiny claws.

After the waitress left us each with a steaming mug of blackish sludge and a pastry whose glaze resembled earwax, Thierry leaned forward. "I filed an incident report with my office and flagged your name on it. It's standard when someone on the team—or a consultant—gets injured."

I dumped in two sugars, and the spoon smoked as it stirred the caustic brew. "Is it supposed to do that?"

"Damn it." She poked at her own mug. "Mervin must be working the kitchen tonight. He's a cherufe." At my blank expression, she made a rolling gesture with her hand. "It's a kind of lava-lizard thing. Once he spat magma on the road, scooped up the molten asphalt and tried to pass it off as the soup du jour. Work crews were patching potholes for days."

I pushed my mug toward the center of the table where it bumped into hers. "If he's that much of a nuisance, then why hasn't he been fired yet?"

She snorted. "Do *you* want to be the one to tell him to hang up his apron?"

"No." I laughed. "I guess not."

Our amusement waned, and Thierry began worrying the bowl of her spoon with her thumb. "Look, Camille, here's the thing. I don't know you, and I don't know your security clearance level, but I know what I saw today. You risked a lot to save your friend, and that makes me think you're one of the good ones."

"Thanks?" My voice rose on the end, making it a question.

"With that in mind," she said, flicking poppy seeds off her pastry one by one, "I'm going to offer you some free advice."

Free advice had a way of costing all the same. "Okay."

"This thing you're hunting?" She cleaned a black dot from under her nail. "It might be Faerie stock. As in the blacklisted, *do not pass go and enter the mortal realm* variety."

The kind so predatory as to not discriminate between fae and mortals, the kind who would make the rivers on Earth run crimson with innocent blood.

My mouth went dry. "That's not possible."

Fae who petitioned for residency in the mortal realm required conclave approval. That didn't mean good fae didn't go bad or that bad fae didn't grease enough palms to slip through the cracks, but there was a subsect of Faerie-born who were never allowed to enter this realm. Most fae called them ancients. Humans would title their arrival apocalypse.

"Nothing is impossible," she contradicted. "Some things are just less plausible than others."

"Magistrate Vause—" I began.

She cut me off by waggling her index finger. "That's all you get for free."

Thinking back to the confrontation in the hall, to her defense of Harlow, I accepted she knew more than I had been told. The only question remaining was could I afford to acquire what she knew? "What will the rest of the information cost?"

"You asked for my blood yesterday." She produced a slender dagger and a charm resembling a charred bird's nest from her satchel. "I'm asking for yours today." The cashier blinked at the blade then went back to picking hairs off his shirt and dropping them on the floor behind the counter. "I'll have to bind you so that the secrets I confide won't be repeated." She poked the ratty twist of straw. "This particular charm is outfitted with a loophole you're probably familiar with since you work high-profile cases. It allows for collaboration between people bound by the same enchantment."

Relief at the familiar gusted through me. She was right. It came standard issue in the arsenal of law enforcement officers and was implemented in cases involving sensitive material. I had subjected myself to such bindings on multiple occasions. Once more wouldn't hurt. Not when she had already whetted my appetite. "I'll do it."

Thierry placed the charm on the tabletop between us then pricked her thumb with the dagger. One drop of blood welled before the cut knit closed, and she smeared it over the charm. "Your turn." She passed me the blade hilt first, and I replicated the gesture. Only my blood continued beading after the requisite drop fell. The wound throbbed as the crimson mixed, and magic slithered a winding path up my arm and throat until it prickled in my lips, binding us to shared secrets.

"Okay." She passed me a napkin. "I'm guessing since my lips feel like I just made out with a porcupine that the charm worked." At my look, she ducked her head and dusted the remains of the spell into her mug where it sizzled and dissolved. "Spellwork isn't my forte. I'm still learning, but I have an excellent teacher."

After wrapping my finger in the thin paper, I settled in while she pulled out a secondary charm and smashed it with the heel of her palm. My ears popped as a privacy spell activated. That one had definitely worked. The restaurant muted around us until the sound of our breathing was all that remained.

"The tethers linking the mortal realm to the fae realm have been severed. I figured it was safe to assume, considering you're with the Earthen Conclave, that you were briefed when the new security protocols were put into place." She waited for my nod. "We're on our own now. That means fae in this world, whether residents or visitors, are subject to conclave law. As I'm sure you're aware, some of the older fae aren't thrilled with the prospect of becoming permanent citizens of Earth. They're bucking the system, and those rebellions are being stamped out as soon as we catch a whiff of them."

"I was flown to Lebanon for debriefing the day after it happened." Kansas that is. I had never been to Faerie myself—my family was Earthborn going back three generations—but even I grasped the magnitude of the situation. We were alone now. Trapped in a world unaware of the existence of fae, but growing so technologically advanced that soon even magic would fail to cloak us from human eyes. If we were discovered, and if mortals reacted to learning there were predators in their midst the way they reacted to most unsettling discoveries, war would break out. Our people would battle—not only the mortals but one another—for control of this world since our native land was lost to us. "I had no idea the tethers were a physical thing that could be cut like string. What sort of fae could be that powerful?"

"Who knows?" Thierry picked at her thumbnail with the single-minded focus of a brain surgeon performing a craniotomy. "Either way it's done now."

I accepted she wasn't going to elaborate and pressed her in another direction. "What does this have to do with Charybdis?"

Her eyebrows lifted, though her gaze remained downcast. "There were other, localized incidents that weren't covered outside of the magistrates' chambers."

Leaning forward, I braced my forearms on the tabletop. "Such as?"

"A few months back a portal opened here in Wink, at the marshal's office actually." Her eyes flicked up at me. "We contained it as fast as we could, but we didn't move to close it quickly enough. Something got through."

"Few fae, even those born in Faerie, can open portals to this realm." That was why losing the tethers had shut down transportation between Earth and Faerie. "From what I've read, theory suggests it requires the cooperation of another party on the side you intend to visit. Someone to open the door for you. That means you need two powerful fae, worlds apart, coordinating their efforts."

"Trust me when I say there was no consenting anchor on this side of the divide." Reddish-brown crust dried around the cuticle of the nail she wouldn't let be. "How it happened doesn't matter as much as the fact that it did."

"How can you say that?" I rapped the table for emphasis. "If there's a fae out there who can bore a tunnel back to Faerie, the conclave will offer amnesty to them if they can do it a second time. That's assuming they aren't recruited by the private sector. A lot of people want to go back, and they'll pay anything—do anything—to get a ticket home."

"That train has left the station." Thierry puffed out her cheeks on an exhale. "The fae responsible has been detained in Faerie and is out of the conclave's reach."

The relief in her voice at the thought of a return trip to Faerie being impossible stumped me. As a legacy, she had a direct familial link to the other realm. Though, as a half-blood, which most Faerie-born scorned, she might have been all too eager for that bridge to burn. For all I knew she had toasted marshmallows in the flames.

"So what you're saying is one fae opened a portal and another one slipped through." The idea it might be Charybdis kicked my pulse up a notch. "Were the two fae cooperating?" That seemed the most likely scenario. "Or was the second incident, the portal breach, a crime of opportunity?"

"We aren't sure." A grim scowl. "With Faerie off the grid, we have no means of confirming their alliance until the second fae is captured here."

I chewed over that bit of information. "What can you tell me about the incident?"

"Not much," she admitted. "We have surveillance footage courtesy of a camera mounted in the hall opposite the office where the breach occurred. The door was open, so it got a clear shot, but the angle is bad, and the quality is crap." Not exactly encouraging. "That said, it shows a humanoid figure stepping through a portal anchored by a closet. It entered the hall, spotted one of the marshals, got spooked, and vanished into thin air."

"How sure are you that this fae and Charybdis are one and the same?"

"I monitored news from around the country for days, waiting to see what it would do." Her fist clenched, and light spilled through her fingers. "The first body surfaced a month later, and the autopsy confirmed the girl had been dead for almost that long."

"The timing could have been a coincidence." Fae were a brutal race. Murder was much less taboo among our people than mortals. "You can't be certain it was the same fae."

"Oh, but I can." She tapped the side of her nose. "I flew out to view the body. The degree of decomposition and exposure to the water made it difficult to parse the smells, but I picked up faint traces of the same scent on the body as I did near the portal."

As powerful as her talents were, I had no reason to doubt Thierry's word. By linking the fae from the portal to the first body, she had established a chain of evidence, because I had tied it and all the others to the same magical signature. "You reported this?"

"To the magistrates, yes." A frown developed. "I also counseled them to call in an expert to work the case. The body wasn't getting any fresher, and I had a feeling that wasn't the end of it." The lines cut deeper into her forehead. "I hate that I was right, but I'm glad they brought you onboard, even if I am curious why Vause sent you here."

"You knew this case wasn't linked to Charybdis." It hit me a second later. "You could tell by the scent."

"Yep." Her lips twisted. "I reached out to Vause when I got a heads up about a consultant visiting the site. I tried to save you a trip, but she made a point of not answering her phone or returning my calls until you had already arrived."

The magistrate had known the death was unrelated to Charybdis, had wanted me in Wink. Staring across the table at the powerful young woman gazing back at me, I had to wonder if this interlude wasn't the entire point. Did that mean Vause had orchestrated my arrival, positioning me in such a way that Thierry's natural curiosity would take over? Or did it mean this comradery was false? That Thierry was Vause's creature? And that our accord was one of many layers in a scheme I would have to peel back to reveal the core of truth?

"Why did you pull out?" I wondered, at the same time realizing this was why her first words to me were that she had been expecting me. She had known I was coming, or someone with a similar talent was, because I was there by her request.

"I'm not a field agent anymore." She grimaced. "I was reassigned elsewhere. My involvement with the portal was a fluke of timing. The magistrates snatched Charybdis out of my hands before I got my fingerprints on the file."

That she still seemed to be working the case without their blessing, I didn't mention. "So I have you to thank for my string of recent consultations."

"Yeah." She winced. "Sorry about that."

"It's no problem." Vause always brought me the mysterious cases in the hopes I could solve with a touch what others struggled to link through evidence. The unspoken agreement she would forward all drowning cases gave me ample opportunity to punish myself. Whatever she thought of my self-flagellation she kept to herself. "This is the job, right?"

"Just know I'm here if you need help." She removed a card from her pocket and pushed it across the table with a finger. "Call if you need anything. Information. References. Backup. Whatever. It's yours."

"I will." I accepted the card and tucked it into my pocket for safekeeping. "I appreciate the offer."

The tension slipped from Thierry's shoulders, and I got the feeling she had accomplished her mission in treating me to coffee at the diner.

"So…Earthen Conclave. They must have been tripping over themselves to enlist someone like you." Her smile didn't reach her eyes. "How did that recruitment letter go? Did they let you say goodbye to your family before they packed you up and shipped you off to one of their training facilities?"

"I didn't get a letter." No one would have thought to send me one. Not with my life expectancy. "I applied to the marshal's program right out of high school. I was drafted from there by Vause after we met on a case I worked in her region."

"You volunteered?" Thierry cocked her head and studied me as though she had never seen me before that moment. "Why?"

"I'm not like the rest of my family." The mention of my otherness made my throat tighten. "I wanted to forge my own path, and the conclave offered to pave the way."

"Hmm." Thierry appeared thoughtful. "I figured someone with your talents would have been scooped up earlier and given fewer choices about it."

She wasn't the only one entitled to her secrets. "Guess I slipped through the cracks."

Never in a million years would the conclave have come looking for me. Even if they had, they would have had trouble locating Aunt Dot's traveling caravan because of the layers of concealment spells she wove around our mobile homes. Gemini were restless souls. Always on the move, always looking ahead to the next thing. Content to leave the past in the past. We enjoyed our own company and preferred our own kind. Untrusting of outsiders, and that went double for those wearing badges. No. The conclave never would have found me if I hadn't wanted to be found.

Aunt Dot had given me an earful when I got my acceptance letter. She saw my attending the academy as penance and still felt like I had turned myself in to the authorities for the crime I hadn't committed as a child. She wasn't wrong. Someone ought to pay for Lori's death. Why not me, the last person to see her alive?

"Guess so." The overhead lights fascinated her for a second while she gathered her thoughts. "Though I suppose we all end up where we're meant to be." Her gaze cut to me. "Fate and all that jazz."

"Sure," I said, though I wasn't sure I agreed with her. Fate and I weren't on speaking terms. An anemic bell tinkled, and a woman with a long brown ponytail entered the diner. The smile proved she wasn't Mrs. Rebec, but her arrival was a sobering reminder of the scene we had left behind. "Do you think Harlow will be safe tonight?"

Thierry's head lifted, and she stared through the large windows positioned across the front of the diner. "We have a guy watching the hotel tonight just in case the widow gets any ideas."

"Good." I rubbed my arms. "She didn't deserve this."

"I hope it serves as a wakeup call for her. A good man died at the sinks because your friend couldn't do her job." Her lips pinched together. "We're lucky Jasper was the only one we lost. Talk to Harlow. Convince her that her limitations need to be documented. A consultant who can't do the job she's hired to do won't have much of a career once her clients catch wind of her record. This is the kind of black mark that never fades."

The impulse to dispute Harlow was a friend while wearing her bracelet caused the words to stick in my throat. The girl was out of her depth, there we agreed, but how likely was a teenager to accept advice from someone she barely knew?

All of the marshals, even Thierry, were so eager to settle the blame on Harlow's shoulders that they didn't seem to grasp how hypocritical it was for them to cast blame. "There might not have been a black mark at all if she had gotten help when it first became obvious she needed it."

"That's part of the problem." Her forehead puckered. "She shouldn't have needed help."

I scoffed, about to call bull. Harlow had been one girl pitted against a monster.

"Hear me out." Thierry splayed her fingers in a peacekeeping gesture. "Merfolk rule the deep. They hold dominion over other aquatic creatures. A mermaid should have had that kraken eating out of the palm of her hand. Or at least been able to corral it until we cleared the scene. But Harlow went in search of the local mermaid pod and instead roused the beast into a killing frenzy." She lowered her hands. "She seems like a nice kid, but…" Her exhale sent a straw wrapper skittering. "I've already filed a report. I can't, in good conscience, allow her to be assigned to another case until she's more forthcoming about her background and her limitations."

A burst of rock music pelted the air, too loud to be coming from outside the privacy spell. My phone's ringtone was much more sedate. That must be Thierry's. "Do you need to get that?"

"Nah." A smile split her cheeks when she read the caller ID. "It's Shaw, but he can wait."

"If something's come up at work…" Food or no food, I was ready to ditch the pretense and call it a night.

"We're off the clock in half an hour." She tapped the cell's screen. "If I pick up, then he'll stick me with being in charge of bringing home dinner, but I know better than to answer him this late in our shift."

"Home," I echoed.

"We're mated." A mischievous glint lit her eyes as she muted her phone. "We've been living together for a whole glorious week."

Of all the things she had told me tonight, this one took the cake. "You *mated* Shaw?"

"Yep." She pocketed her phone and pulled out a slim wallet. "For better or worse, he's all mine."

That explained a lot and nothing at all. Incubi mated? For how long? To what end? Thierry must be a bold woman to trust an incubus with her heart. I got the feeling if he ever strayed, she would light him up like the Fourth of July. Maybe that made him the bold one.

After tossing a few bills on the table for a tip, she glanced up at me. "Will you be leaving tomorrow?"

"I should have been gone today. There's nothing left for me to do here." Harlow ought to get going too. Tonight's confrontation wouldn't have happened if she had gone home on schedule. "Have the boy's parents been located?"

"No." She flagged down the waitress and signaled for the check. "Not yet. He's not local. We ruled out that possibility. He could be a runaway, but with a mouth full of metal, I doubt it. Braces require a lot of maintenance, and his were pristine." She paid the tab despite my protests. "We'll find his family. Don't worry about that." She slid out of the booth. "Come on. I'll walk you back."

We hit the hotel lobby in time to hear the screams.

CHAPTER SIX

Spine-covered rats poured like spilled marbles across the tile floor, and I hopped an instinctive step back until I spotted Harlow struggling in their midst. Nails clacking, they scurried toward the exit Thierry and I moved to block. Their pointy shoulders were packed so tightly they formed a living carpet, and Harlow flailed her arms and legs as she rode them Aladdin-style across the lobby. Every time she managed to get a hand or foot on the floor, one of them bit her wrists or stabbed her ankles until she recoiled and the procession continued. The overnight clerk quivered on top of her desk shrieking and doing some terrified variation of the *gotta pee* dance. That accounted for the screams.

"Cam," Harlow squeaked, catching sight of me. "Thank the gods. Get these things off me. Their spines effing hurt."

"Hold on." Thierry slung an arm out in front of my chest. "Let me think."

The incessant screaming made my back teeth ache. "What are those things?"

"They're hedgies—hedgehogs." She glanced at me and lowered her arm. "Or they would be if they weren't fae. These little guys are igel, and they're usually harmless."

"Can we hurry this up?" Harlow kicked at one gnawing on the heel of her shoe. "I feel like shish kebab over here."

"Why are they fixated on Harlow?" Not a one of the creatures had given us a second glance except maybe to wonder how to skitter past without sacrificing their cargo.

A sigh puffed out Thierry's cheeks. "Jasper Rebec was an igel."

"So this could be his family." Sent to fetch the one his widow blamed for his death.

"Yeah." She patted her pockets. "I don't want to hurt them. Grief makes us all lose our heads."

"Can you hurry this up?" Harlow asked with a yelp as a spine pierced her palm.

"Looks like you could use some help," an earthy voice rumbled.

A man leaned against the far wall with a toothpick stuck to his bottom lip. I hadn't noticed him at first, what with the rodent infestation, but I sure saw him now. Cord Graeson had followed me—*us*—to Texas. I would have recognized the scowl even if I hadn't noticed the black ink forest sprouting from his wrists to spread up his forearms.

"We appreciate the offer," Thierry drawled, "but looks can be deceiving."

His casual lean, his serene expression, set me on edge. He had been more honest gripped by his anger and grief. This cool-headed Graeson seemed dangerous, like he was a spring wound too tight, ready to burst into motion at the least provocation.

"How long have you been standing there?" A purse of his lips confessed nothing, and I stepped around Thierry, approaching him with caution. "Were you going to let them roll away with her?"

Eyes the color of walnuts striated by the green of summer grasses shifted onto Harlow. "No." The reluctance in the word didn't convince me.

A buzzing noise spooked the hedgies, who curled into balls with a hiccup of sound. Thierry leapt into action, pulling a black stick—a marker?—from her pocket and drawing a circle around the stunned hedgies. "Harlow." Thierry clasped forearms with her when she glanced up, and then hauled her to her feet. "Get out of the circle. Don't smudge the line." Harlow stepped over the black line and backed to my side. Thierry spoke a Word, and an invisible barrier rose, penning the hedgies. She pocketed the marker and dusted her hands. "Easy-peasy. I'll call a cleanup crew."

Harlow pulled a slim phone from the rear pocket of her shorts. Her cell's vibrations must have been what startled the hedgies. Her mouth pinched at the corners when the screen illuminated. "I have to return this call." She crossed the lobby, pushed a button and started pacing. "Magistrate Vause." Her knees locked and complexion paled. "Y-yes, ma'am." Her head swung toward me.

"Camille is right here." She extended the phone, careful not to let our fingers brush. "It's for you."

I held the phone to my right ear and then covered my left to better hear over the protesting hedgies. "Ellis speaking."

"Why aren't you answering your phone?"

Short and to the point is our Seelie Magistrate.

"I went out for coffee." I braced against the snap in her voice. "I forgot my phone."

"I've heard of twenty-four-hour coffee shops," she mused in a frosty tone. "Here I thought it referenced their hours, not the number of hours customers are lost once crossing their threshold."

The explanation she hinted at wanting but wouldn't ask for outright caused the conversation to peter out into an awkward quiet. Her silent demand for an explanation had me digging in my heels. The conclave didn't own me. I was an employee who performed services for pay, not an indentured servant who had to snap to attention and report on command.

"We have a survivor," Vause announced in a cool, clear voice.

"Are you certain she escaped Charybdis?" I pressed the speaker tighter against my ear. "The victim in Wink was just a boy in the wrong place at the wrong time. He wasn't one of ours."

"The certainty is yours to determine. I wouldn't dream of doing your job for you." A prim response. "You will have to visit the girl and get the answers we both require."

Residual imprints faded fast on a living person. As they recovered, the resurgence of their own magic wiped away any foreign signatures. "How reliable is she?"

"The girl is ten. Elizabeth McKenna." Leather creaked on her end. "I want you to talk to her."

"Sure." My heart pounded faster. "Where?"

"The incident occurred in Falco, Alabama. We'll need a diver. Bring Harlow with you." Metal groaned as though she were reclining in a desk chair. "And, Camille? When I say I want you to speak with her, I mean I want Lori."

Lori.

Harlow's phone slid through my limp fingers. Only her quick reflexes kept it from clattering on the tiles. She ended the call with Vause. I didn't have the stomach left for pleasantries.

Graeson straightened, arms hanging loose as if ready to catch me should my knees buckle. "What's happened?"

Head light as a balloon ready to float off my shoulders, I shut my eyes and let the pain wash over me. Nothing could dam the swell of hurt, and I wasn't fool enough to try. Better to weather the surge now than fight to keep my head above water later.

"Cam?"

"Pack a bag." I opened my eyes, held Harlow's wary gaze. "We leave in a half hour."

A sharp nod, a hardening of her jaw, and she dashed toward the elevators.

I should have called out, asked her to hold the door for me so I could join her, but instead I nodded to Thierry—deep in conversation about the logistics of humane igel removal—and exited the building. Beneath a heavy moon, I stood as a speck on the sidewalk of no significance to the celestial bodies twinkling above me and found my center. The glitter of stars was proof the dark blanket of my grief did not encompass the world, and I could not allow it to envelope me.

"You didn't answer my question."

The unwelcome interruption growled over my shoulder splintered the moment of clarity almost within my reach. "I should pack my things."

"Are you ignoring me because I'm a warg?" A hint of bitterness. "Would you speak to me as an equal if I were fae?"

"My issue is not your species," I said, voice weary. "You're too close to the case to act rationally."

"Do you have any siblings?" He wielded the question like a blade. "All I had was Marie." The sentiment cut deep. "Survive a loss of that magnitude and then we can talk about acting rationally."

Too late to conceal my flinch, I smoothed the gesture into a shrug. "This isn't about me."

Head cocked to one side, nostrils widening, Graeson cataloged a piece of me I hadn't meant to share with him. Old hurts roiled in me. I must stink of emotion to such a sensitive nose as his.

"You might as well tell me why the magistrate called," he coaxed, his voice a dark promise. "I had the resources to locate you once. I can again." Gold eclipsed his irises. "Marie was my sister.

She died on Chandler pack land. As her brother, as beta, I have a right to this hunt."

My tongue pressed against the back of my front teeth. As much as I might wish otherwise, he had as much right to hunt Charybdis as I did, maybe more. His earlier stab in the dark had drawn heart's blood. Had Marie been my sister, I would be in his place. No question. It was instinct to punish those who harmed what we loved. For Graeson, that meant Charybdis. In my case, the only person to blame was me.

"There's a girl." My throat scraped raw. "A witness."

"Where?" His hand dipped into his pocket, emerging with a ring of keys looped around his forefinger.

I bit the inside of my cheek and made a decision. "How did you get here?"

"I drove that gray SUV by the portico." He showed me the fob with a familiar rental agency logo affixed to its surface. "Why?"

"Great." I hustled past, the time for dawdling over. "Then you have plenty of room for Harlow."

Putting the two of them in the same car meant I could keep an eye on both. It was a win/win that promised Graeson only the access I decided to allow him and Harlow protection should the igel mount another effort against her.

His fist clenched. "What about your car?"

"All they had available was a subcompact." It was cute as a button, but tight even for a quick trip to the airport once you factored in two women and two sets of luggage. "You can drive Harlow, and I'll meet you both at the airport. We can travel the rest of the way together."

A thoughtful pause while Graeson no doubt weighed the compromise I offered against the effort it would require to uncover the same information from one of his resources. "All right. You have a deal."

"Great." I hesitated, glanced back at him. "Are you waiting down here?"

"Unless you're inviting me up." He tossed his keys, caught them.

"I won't be long." I resumed walking. "Wait here, save yourself the trip."

"Make it quick." A glint in his eye. "Or I might make you the same offer."

The subtle warning nudged me up to my room where I collected my belongings and packed with less care than usual. I was wrapping my laptop cord when Harlow breezed in ten minutes later with her bags in hand. While performing one last sweep of the bed and floor, I explained our travel arrangements.

Ushering her into the hall ahead of me, I hesitated with my hand on the doorknob.

"Ready?" she prompted.

To resurrect my dead twin sister for the purpose of conducting an interview? "Yeah. Sure."

Not at all.

CHAPTER SEVEN

Between the late flight and the car ride, and Graeson appointing himself our driver, I managed three hours of sleep before we arrived at a two-star hotel in Andalusia, Alabama. Harlow, Graeson and I checked in then went our separate ways. I headed to my room for a shower and a change of clothes. At this point, I wanted the food I still hadn't eaten more than I wanted a power nap before facing Vause.

Dressed in a black pantsuit with a white ruffled shirt, I twisted my hair into a tight bun at the back of my head then left the room and rode the elevator down to the lobby. I stepped off and bumped right into Graeson, who stood with his feet braced apart and arms crossed over his chest, waiting. His hands shot out to steady me, and even after I stopped wobbling, he was slow to release me.

The damp hair slicking to his scalp reminded me of the first time we met and the circumstances that had brought us together. I stepped out of his reach and headed across the lobby where leftovers from the free continental breakfast were being picked over.

"Where do you think you're going?" His voice slid over my shoulder, his breath warm at my ear.

"I'm starving." I pressed a fist to my gut. "I'm heading where the food is."

He hooked my arm and spun me around. Once my head stopped whirling, I realized he was marching me out the front entryway.

"What are you—?" I struggled to get free. "The food is that way."

"No." His rough palm cupped my jaw and turned my head. "The *real* food is that way."

The familiar red Shoney's sign glowed from across the street, and my stomach gurgled. All-you-can-eat eggs, bacon, pancakes and home-style fried potatoes. That sounded so much better than bottomless orange juice and kiddie cereal.

"Wait." I glanced behind us. "Where's Harlow?"

"Already gone. Got picked up five minutes ago." He tugged on my arm to get me moving. "She's got orders to search the lake for evidence of occupation."

The odds Charybdis had stayed put after a failed abduction were slim. He hadn't managed to elude authorities this long by taking chances.

"We should probably get moving too," I said weakly. We stood at the entrance to the restaurant, and Graeson pushed open the door, allowing the scents of fried meats and waffles cooking to breeze past us. My mouth filled with water, and I glanced back at him. "You don't play fair."

He placed his hand at the small of my back and pressed. "Fair doesn't taste like bacon."

I couldn't argue with that logic.

A waitress greeted us, saw the bacon lust in our eyes and showed us to a table. While she fixed our drinks, we hit the buffet. I grabbed a little of everything and a lot of the fried potatoes. Those tiny cubes were my favorite thing. Beside me, Graeson piled mountains of ham, sausage patties and links, and crisp bacon strips on his plate. He caught me goggling at the sheer volume of meat and added a scoop of potatoes to his plate.

Shaking my head, I took my breakfast and found our table. Graeson sat at the same time, waiting until I had taken the first bite before tucking into his meal. I didn't stand on formalities. I was shoveling potatoes and eggs into my mouth almost as fast as he was inhaling sausage links. After I had cleaned my plate, I sat back, eyeing his stack of country ham with a fork in hand, all the while wondering how quick his reflexes were.

"Don't even think about it." He scooted his meal closer to his side of the table. "There's a whole buffet out there."

"I don't think I can move," I admitted. Eating so much so fast had made me lethargic.

He rose with liquid grace. "Sit tight."

Sitting wasn't a problem. It was the getting up while carrying a sack of Idaho's best in my stomach that would be the issue. I shut my eyes and basked in the sensation of fullness. I jumped when an arm brushed my shoulder. I jerked upright, but it was only Graeson. He had leaned over me to place my plate on the table, which set off fluttering in a stomach already feeling twitchy. Having a predator at my back wasn't helping my digestion.

"Here." He lingered in my personal space before withdrawing. "That should tide you over until dinner."

"Dinner?" Fork in hand, the better to stab him at the least provocation, I examined what he had chosen for me. "What about lunch?"

"Lunch is the least dependable meal of the day." He reclaimed his seat and lifted his fork, again waiting for me to take a bite before he began eating. "It's smarter to fuel up now in case we don't get another chance."

The mountain of potatoes loomed, and though I shouldn't have kept scooping them in, I did. I only stopped after noticing Graeson's attention on my lips as I chewed. I fumbled the fork and grabbed a napkin. "What?" I wiped my mouth. "Did I get grease on my face?"

Voice gone coarse, he ground out a single word. "No."

There wasn't enough liquid left in my glass to wet my throat when he looked at me with that potent mix of grief and guilt I understood too well. Living, even for a moment, after someone you loved had died, carved up your insides. I drained the juice and still felt parched. "I need a refill." I pushed my chair back. "Do you want anything?"

Shadows darkening his eyes, he shook his head, gaze falling to the condensation beading on his water glass.

"Graeson..." I began, not sure where to go from there, comforting others an unfamiliar task.

"We don't have long." He flicked off the droplets one by one. "Vause is expecting you."

Easing from my seat, I approached the beverage station and poured more orange juice, drained the glass and then repeated the process. A prickle of awareness swept over me, and I turned. Graeson sat at the table, fork on his napkin, waiting for me, the ghost of his sister haunting his gaze.

The drive to Falco was silent but for the low buzz of the radio, the car filled with things neither of us was saying. I had turned to answering emails on my phone to distract myself from the price I was about to pay in order to purchase another scrap of information that might help us end this man hunt before another girl was taken. Graeson's voice, after such heavy quiet, startled me into dropping my cell in my lap.

"You reek of grief." He killed the radio. "The closer we get to town, the more intense it becomes."

Suppressing the urge to sniff myself, I wrinkled my nose. "I'm thinking of the victims."

It wasn't an outright lie. It was a miracle this one girl out of so many had escaped. I hadn't stopped wondering what made her different since Vause told me about her. My job put me in direct contact with victims, their families and friends. Meeting a survivor? That was almost enough to buoy my introspective mood.

"That's not it. You've been distraught since you spoke to Vause." He cut his gaze my way. "Who is Lori?"

The bottom fell out of my stomach. "You were eavesdropping?"

"My hearing is superior to yours," he stated matter-of-factly. "I can't help what I overhear."

He sounded all torn up over it too.

"Don't mention her name again." My voice trembled. Grief. Rage. I wasn't sure there was a line separating the two where she was concerned.

Graeson got quiet, but it was the unsettling peace of a man deep in thought. I didn't trust it.

Hours later we hit the strip qualifying Falco as a town and parked on the curb in front of a faded meter with crackled glass. Blinds slatted three of the storefronts' windows. A "For Lease" sign had been taped to the door of each empty space. The fourth, the one on the end, was papered over with old newsprint. If I tilted my head just right, the pane glimmered with a sheen of magic. Nothing about it advertised the purpose of the space, but two people entered and four left before we reached the door.

After stepping across the threshold, glamour flared behind my eyes and faded to leave green images superimposed on my retinas. We had stepped off the mundane street and into a gleaming lobby with a wide receptionist desk manned by a dryad wearing a handful of leaves artfully arranged into a halter-style dress. Other fae lounged in over-plush chairs or helped themselves to a food-service station that smelled spicy and rich with heated beverages.

The scent of fresh chai brewing made my mouth water. "What is this place?"

"This is safe house two-four-nine," a chilly voice intoned. "It's a low-level facility for fae assimilating into the area after forceful relocation from their home territory."

The clipped voice at my ear made me jump. Throat tight, I propped my lips into a smile before I turned.

A petite woman stood behind me. At five-five I wasn't tall, but I towered over her. Pale blonde hair a few shades lighter than mine was swept into a bun so tight I could probably bounce a quarter off her coif. Cornflower-blue eyes swept over me with anticipation, as if expecting me to yank Lori out of my jacket pocket. Two slender men outfitted in black fatigues accompanied her. Their sharp eyes never stopped scanning the area. Their palms rested on the hilts of swords they made no effort to hide.

"Magistrate Vause." Speaking her name broke sweat down my spine. "I didn't expect to see you."

Trepidation had kept me from reading between the lines. I should have anticipated she would choose to witness a talent I was reluctant to use. The conclave liked to keep tabs on its resources, after all. Especially the underutilized ones.

"This matter requires special attention." A practical smile. "And here I am."

She rarely left the outpost the Northeastern Conclave called home. I glanced behind her, almost expecting to see her Unseelie counterpart. Magistrates came in pairs—one Seelie and one Unseelie—as a means of keeping the balance between their two factions. As a Seelie myself, it was natural she would be my contact person. But the absence of her counterpart pricked at the worry budding in the back of my mind.

Thierry had warned me that Charybdis was the product of a portal breach, and that changed everything. He was a dangerous fae preying on other fae. Wouldn't both parties be equally invested in seeing the killer captured in the interest of appeasing their partisans? He had targeted both Seelie and Unseelie, as well as Earth natives like Graeson's sister.

To distract myself from what was to come, I glanced around. "It's busy for a safe house, isn't it?"

"As far as the mortals are concerned, it's Tuna Tuesday at the homeless shelter." She extended her arm, and I braced for impact before shaking her hand. Electricity swam through my veins and fisted my heart in a vise. "Camille." Her lips curved upward, but her gaze remained distant and hard. "Despite the circumstances, it is good to see you. We miss you in Maine."

"Tennessee is nice. I like the mountains." I retreated closer to Graeson, which earned me an arched eyebrow from him. "I like the marshal's office I work out of now." Remembering my manners, I forced out, "I appreciate your recommendation. It went a long ways toward convincing the office they could afford me."

"It was nothing. I'm pleased your new environment suits you. For the time being. I know how much your family enjoys travel." Vause held out her hand, and one of her guards squirted hand sanitizer into her palm. The scent of strawberry lemonade tickled my nose. "Who is this? Did you take a cab from the hotel?" She massaged in the liquid, gaze raking over Graeson with no small amount of disdain before turning back to me. "Ask your driver to wait in the car."

"No offense, ma'am—" and he made it sound plenty offensive, "—but the conclave governs fae." A feral grin. "I'm not fae."

Wargs were, in polite terms, human genetic mutations. The same as vampires. Magic was in the mix too, but it was Earth magic. Not Faerie-born.

"This is a conclave-owned facility." Smugness radiated through the rub of her hands. "And I am asking you to leave."

In a heartbeat, one of the guards drew his sword and pressed it to Graeson's throat. The warg didn't blink. If anything, his impending decapitation appeared to bore him. I wasn't half so blasé about blood spilling without cause.

"The previous victim—" a cold title for a girl who had been Graeson's sister, "—was killed on Chandler pack land." I glanced between the wicked sharp blade, the disinterested warg and the magistrate with glittering eyes. "Mr. Graeson, as a member of the Chandler pack, has rights under the Native Species of Magical Origins Act."

Some of the sparkle left Vause's gaze. "So he does." A cutting glance from her and the guard sheathed his blade. "Very well, Mr. Graeson. You may stay." Vause pretended interest in her nails. "You may observe Camille's technique with me."

I flinched at the punishment. It didn't go unnoticed by Graeson. The last thing I wanted was for him to witness what I was about to do. Vause knew it, and she had offered him a front-row seat.

"We can't detain the girl much longer." Vause strode down the hall with the confidence of someone who expected her orders to be followed. One guard accompanied her. The other, the one who had drawn on Graeson, hung back to babysit him. She snapped her fingers. "Camille?"

"Coming." I reached her side in a few quick strides. She hadn't been waiting. Her legs were just that short. "What you're asking me to do…" I wiped my damp palms on my pants. "I don't know if…"

"You can do this." She sounded more confident in my abilities than I ever had been. "It's one of your gifts. To perfect it, you must practice it."

I sucked down a shuddering breath, seconds from pleading with her to let me off the hook or to find someone else to conduct the interview. She must have sensed my crumbling resolve, because she guided me into a small room and shut the door behind us. It locked. The interior was dark, and the front wall was made entirely of glass. A two-way mirror.

The view made my chest ache. A figure wrapped in a fuzzy canary-yellow blanket sat on a chair bolted to the floor. All the furniture in the interrogation room was secured, but the stark contrast of that quivering mound of fabric worn soft by multiple washings and the sterile room made me cringe. All I saw to confirm someone was underneath were the tips of two slender fingers holding it in place.

"She hasn't spoken a word since she was recovered." Vause peered at the girl with a frown cutting her mouth. "We need to find out what she knows before shock erodes her memory." A grimace. "Children are so resilient."

The line, delivered with such clipped precision, didn't strike me as Vause relaying a comforting thought as much as her admonishing a flaw in the child's makeup. But she was right. It was now or never, and the cost to me paled in comparison to the loss of more children.

And yet the echo of a small girl trapped in my bones trembled at the thought of being resurrected this way.

"I'll do what I can." I held her black-lashed stare. "No promises."

The gleam returned to her eyes. "Do you need a moment?"

"I— Yeah. I do." I seized the opportunity with both hands. "I haven't done this since…"

Not since the day she walked into the marshal's office where I worked, pointed at me and left the building, clearly expecting me to follow. I went from Northeast Conclave marshal to Earthen Conclave agent overnight, and Vause had led the recruitment charge. The other magistrates, a circle of ten, had demanded a show of my powers. They documented my abilities and then ripped my body through the change without waiting for my protest.

No doubt if I failed to shift on my own now, then Vause knew similar methods for drawing Lori into the open. I shivered at the thought.

"Very well. You will enter the interrogation room through there." She pointed out a door to my left. "I'll be overseeing the interview with her parents and Mr. Graeson from a second private room behind the opposing two-way mirror."

Looking over my shoulder literally. Great. "Okay."

After she left, my back hit the wall, and I sank to the floor. I banged my head against the glass until the base of my skull rang. It didn't help. I kept Lori tucked so deep in my memories that pulling her out made me physically ill. But asking Vause for help would be worse. So much worse.

Come out, come out, wherever you are...

Minutes passed. A half hour elapsed. Maybe an hour. Sweat drenched my face and clung to my upper lip. The tapping of my foot sparked a headache, but I couldn't seem to hold still. My skin itched and burned. That tightness reminded me of sun-drenched days and warm summer nights. I had spent every summer of my early childhood caravanning with relatives through the Great

Smoky Mountains. I filled my lungs, aching for the sweet bite of spruce trees.

Just like that, my gut wrenched. My bones ached in time with my heartbeat, and my marrow tingled. The change compressed me, smashed me into a form that ought to be too small to hold an adult. I sat on the floor, legs crossed and trembling, and gazed into my reflection. My chest hurt. I don't know how long I had been rubbing it, but finger marks reddened the fragile skin.

Mom used to say Geminis were born as sets of identical twins because we practiced mimicry even in the womb. The first talent we develop is the ability to read the powers of others. It's a survival mechanism. We're not a strong breed. We're not much more resilient than humans in terms of strength and durability, which means it's critical for us to surround ourselves with strong allies and to learn how to identify magic that complements those around us.

The second gift we receive, at around the age of three, is the ability to assume the appearance of our twin. In essence, we mimic ourselves through that connection. It's a fail-safe, an emergency reset in case we absorb a power that doesn't burn out or sprout appendages that won't unsprout. We aren't doppelgangers. We don't create fetches, constructs of glamour and shadow that resembles a person or creature. What we do isn't a complete transformation. It's a temporary augmentation, a skimming of the best qualities of another fae that we then absorb into ourselves for a short time. And when we get stuck in our own bodies, we assume the form of our twin. After shifting back to ourselves from that point, we're, well, ourselves.

Except my reset was as broken as I was. Lori was frozen in time. Never changing, never aging…

The change redoubled its efforts to compress me, squeezing my torso so hard I was amazed when my head didn't pop off.

In the mirror, my ash-blonde hair lightened to platinum. The shoulder-length cut grew to the small of my back. My narrow face plumped with the roundness of childhood. My turbulent eyes rounded with innocence, and pink splashed my cheeks with enthusiasm. When I stood, I was the height I had been at the age of eight. The black slacks and dress shirt had vanished. So had my boots. A nightgown printed with fat moons and grinning stars brushed my ankles. My throat constricted as I stared at my own reflection. I lifted a child-sized hand and waved to myself.

"Hi, Lori," I said in a breathless voice that sounded fresh off a playground.

But Lori was gone. There was only me and the magical imprint stamped on my brain from the last time we had practiced *becoming,* as Mom called it.

I entered the interrogation room, and the victim didn't bat an eyelash. Circling the desk, I sat in the chair positioned across from hers, propped my elbows on the tabletop then pressed my fists into my cheeks.

"I'm Cam." I started swinging my legs. "What's your name?"

Elizabeth's pale brown eyes lifted, but she didn't speak.

"I live in Tennessee." My elbow slipped. "Where are you from?"

"What are you?" she asked quietly.

"I'm fae, like you."

Her head tilted. "You're not really a kid."

I pressed my palms flat to the table. "How can you tell?"

"Your eyes." The fabric slid off the back of her head to reveal burnt-auburn curls. "They look old, sad."

Perceptive girl.

My toes skidded across the floor. "You're right." I sat up straighter. "This isn't how I usually look."

She leaned forward, and the blanket shifted down around her elbows. "Are you a shifter or something?"

"Kind of." I played with the strap of my nightgown. "Have you heard of Geminis before?"

Flattened curls bounced around her shoulders when she shook her head. "What are those?"

I stuck out my arm. "Let me see your hand, and I'll show you." She hesitated. "I won't hurt you." Skin-to-skin contact worked for this particular trick. Blood was only required when I wanted to initiate a change. "I give you my word."

Tiny white teeth pressed into her bottom lip, and she clasped palms with me. A hot rush of energy stung my fingers.

"Let me guess." I screwed up my face like I required concentration. "You're a...*phoenix*."

A phoenix wearing a fifth-tier glamour, one who had, without a doubt, been touched by Charybdis's magic.

"Am I right?" I prompted when the girl's face crumpled.

Her species explained her perception. She had an old soul. She might have been reborn hundreds of times before this life. Perhaps it also explained how she had survived Charybdis. The wisdom of previous lives resided in that tiny head of hers. What it didn't explain was her reaction.

"How did you know?" She touched her arm. "Can you see through my glamour?"

I always knew when glamour was in use, but I couldn't see beneath it so much as guess, depending on species, what features a particular fae might want hidden.

Phoenix were flawless, human in appearance until they embraced their inner firebird. I bet myself a dunk in the lake Elizabeth hadn't required glamour prior to meeting Charybdis.

"It's just something all Geminis can tell."

"That's cool I guess." She studied me. "So what do *you* really look like?"

"Like this, but older." I wanted to smile at the chipped purple paint on my fingernails. "This is how my sister looked the last time I saw her."

"When was that?"

Thirteen years ago. I had been splintered longer than Elizabeth had been alive. "A long time ago."

"Did something happen to her? Is that why you're so sad?"

"She..." Hot tears prickled my eyes. "She drowned when we were about your age."

The little girl shrugged her blanket back up around her neck. "I almost drowned too."

Yanking my thoughts away from Lori, I pushed out the right questions. "How did you get away?"

"I set the marsh on fire." The blanket wriggled higher until her hair vanished beneath it. "The monster screamed, and it ran away."

Adrenaline dumped over my head. "You saw it?"

An ID on the killer would crack the case wide open. The surveillance tip was good, but this would be gold.

"It was so pretty," she whispered. "I just wanted to pet it."

Pet it? That was not what I expected her to say. "Tell me everything you remember."

"We were on a camping trip with my Junior Conclave troop. There was swamp on either side of the path we were hiking, and Mrs. Dial said not to go out there or the gators would eat me." The blanket shivered. "But I heard… I thought the gators were after it. I didn't want it to get eaten." Her fingertips vanished into the folds of material. "I waited until Mrs. Dial stopped to help a kid tie his shoes, and then I sneaked into the swamp. That's where I saw it."

"It?"

"A white horse."

Chills swept down my spine. That piece of evidence was damning on so many levels. "Did you?"

"I didn't see any gators, but I thought maybe its foot was stuck in the mud. That happened to my friend Jenny's pony once when it got out of its pen." Her breathy voice trembled. "I walked over, and it nuzzled my arm like it wanted a pet. So I did. I petted it, but its fur was sticky. I couldn't get my hand back. I started yanking hard, and the horse got mad. It started walking toward the water." Liquid eyes peered out at me. "It was a trick. The horse wasn't stuck in the mud at all."

Confirmation of his hunting pattern was as good as confirmation of species. I knew what he was, or what he pretended to be. How could Charybdis be both the humanoid fae in the surveillance video and the horse? Kelpies—and she had just given me a textbook description of one—weren't shapeshifters. "Is that when you set the marsh on fire?"

Elizabeth stared into her lap. "I couldn't let go of it." Her eyes filled with tears. "It couldn't let go of me either, but the fire scared it, and…" She raised her left hand, the one she had touched earlier with sad eyes.

Magic peppered the air, and her personal glamour vanished. Her hand did too. She had been amputated at the wrist. Her fair skin was puckered and pink where it disappeared into a bandage capping her arm.

Dull shock roared in my ears. She had survived, but gods it had cost her. "Can you show me where you found the horse?"

"No." A violent sob wracked her body, and she dissolved into tears. "P-p-please don't make me go back. *Please*. I don't want to see him again. Please."

Heart breaking, I rushed around the table and wrapped my arms around Elizabeth. At first, we were of a similar height. Then pain radiated down my limbs as the bones elongated and skin stretched. I smoothed her hair and rocked her while jagged magic buzzed through my body, transforming me until the world took on a different perspective. Lori was gone—my hold on her had slipped. I was Camille now, but the girl didn't care. She just wanted to be held and told everything would be all right.

As much as I wanted to speak the words, I kept them in where they couldn't make me a liar.

The door burst open behind us, and a couple smelling of burning leaves charged into the room. The woman's hair smoldered, red and glittery, as she scooped up Elizabeth and cradled the girl against her chest.

A thin crimson rim flickered around the irises of the brown-eyed man who must be Mr. McKenna. When he spoke, smoke poured from his mouth. "She's suffered enough."

"Yes," I agreed. "She has."

The couple exited with their daughter nestled tight in a blanket I was now willing to bet was flame-retardant. I stood there, expecting Vause to bustle in behind them and critique my performance in her detached way. When she failed to appear, I sat back down and braced my forearms on the table that was much easier to reach now.

I must have dozed off, because when a deep throat cleared, I jerked upright and wiped drool off the corner of my mouth. Time had passed, but I wasn't sure how much. A minute. An hour. However long it had been, it hadn't been long enough to rid my eyelids of their sandpaper texture. "What?"

Graeson set a paper cup of steaming chai on the table and scooted it toward me with a finger. "Drink that."

After our morning spent inhaling carbs together, I didn't argue. I wrapped both hands around the paper cup and let the warmth thread through me. I brought it to my lips and moaned while knocking back the best latte I had ever drank. He watched me lick my lips with unsettling attentiveness. I tapped the rim with my fingertip. “You didn’t have to do this.”

“I know,” he said, a world of meaning saturating those two words, but I was too exhausted to ring the intent from them.

With the cup drained, I searched for a trash can but came up empty. “Where’s Vause?”

“Otherwise occupied.” He took the opposite chair, the better to lock stares with me. “This is why you were grieving.”

There was no point in lying. He would smell that too. “Yes.”

His jaw clenched. “Vause had no right to ask you to do this.”

“We got our ID.” I wasn’t ready to discuss Lori with him yet. “Now we know Charybdis is a kelpie.”

Kelpies were water spirits who most often appeared in the guise of a black or white horse. They lured victims to them by faking injury or some other *poor me* ploy. Once there was a foal born of a kelpie father and siren mother that ensnared victims with its song. Regardless of the mechanism, the stories always ended the same way. Kelpies coaxed their victims onto their backs, carried their riders into the depths of the lake or river where they hunted, and then feasted on them.

The problem being Charybdis was roaming, which wasn’t normal kelpie behavior. Neither was wasting a kill. The only damage these victims had sustained was the loss of a hand or forearm. He was allowing them to touch him, hauling them into the water to drown them, and then leaving the bodies. Why?

“Don’t stonewall me,” he growled. “For gods’ sake, Ellis, look at me.”

Compassion waited for me in his gaze, its weight pressed me down until I couldn’t have lifted my head if I wanted. Instead I picked at the cardboard cuff around my cup. “How much did you see?”

His silence told me he had witnessed the entire production.

“What do you want from me?” A mirthless laugh died in my throat. “What do you expect me to say?”

“Does it get better?” His voice scraped up his throat. “Does it ever…?”

“No.” The unshed tears in my eyes fell. “The hole in your chest is always gaping. Nothing else will fill it. No one who didn’t know the one you lost will understand.” I took a slow breath. “People will tell you how to grieve, what to feel, and how long you're allowed to hurt. A few weeks, a couple of months, and that's it. The empathy runs dry. Your grief becomes the elephant in the room that tramples anyone who tries to take that pain away." Harsh laughter burned my chest. "Then you move on, or you do such a damn fine acting job others think you have, and then they sigh with relief. Tears get packed away, the hurt gets hidden." I cut my finger on the drink's lid then pressed it against the cardboard until it stopped bleeding. "Everyone supports your loss until they're tired of how lost you really are."

A warm thumb swiped across my cheek, smudging the wet streaks. "You can't heal until you let yourself grieve."

I sucked in a sharp breath. I hadn't seen him move. "I can't go back to that place." My lungs forgot how to expand until he lowered his hand. "I might never climb out again."

Shadows darkened his eyes, but he nodded. He understood. His pain was fresh enough for him to feel the same ragged scars on his heart as those decorating mine. Though he did a better job of concealing them than I had at this stage.

"What happened to Lori?" He braced a hand on the back of my chair, close enough his heat radiated through my spine. "How did she die?"

The raw ache in his voice, a mirror to my own, caused me to come undone for the first time since I sobbed on my mother's lap, salt burning the cut on my foot, blood smearing her bare knee, and I found myself talking without making the conscious decision to confide in him.

"The ocean..." I rubbed my throat like it might loosen it. "Every summer my extended family gathered, ditched the RVs and hiked through the Great Smoky Mountains. It was tradition. Lori and I—we loved it." The weight of him at my back made speaking easier. "One summer Mom got a wild hair to see the ocean. It had been so long, she said, and everyone ought to see the Gulf at least once."

"What happened?" A soft question with rounded edges that still managed to slice through me.

"We sneaked out of our parents' trailer and ran down to the beach. It was late. Past midnight. We were alone." My voice trembled. "I cut my foot on a shell. Lori was running ahead of me.

I couldn't catch up to her. She was always faster than me." I had to try a few times before the rest came rushing out. "She splashed into the surf. I told her not to, but she waded out into the water. I didn't go in after her because I didn't want my foot to burn." Fresh tears welled. "She was standing there. Right there. In front of me. And then she was gone." I wiped my hands over my cheeks. "I couldn't see her, but the screams…"

"Ellis..." His hands curved around my shoulders. "That's enough. You don't have to share any more."

Too late. It was too late to stop the torrent of memory from spilling between us. The story wanted to be told, like spitting out the words would somehow absolve me for my part in Lori's death. "I ran to find my parents." I stared at the empty seat in front of me, picturing Lori sitting there bundled up and safe instead of Elizabeth. "I left her alone. I didn't even try to help her. I just…ran." Her screams had chased me back to the campsite. "Mom had already noticed us missing. She always checked in on us during the night, like she was afraid we might vanish if she didn't make sure we were tucked safely into bed each time she passed our room. They saw me and heard Lori. They ran to the beach, but she was gone." I wiped my nose. "We never recovered her body."

A hard note entered his voice, and it sounded dangerously close to a reprimand. "That's why you're working these cases."

Admitting it made me sound even more broken, even more screwed up, because I refused to let go of the past. Rationally, I knew no matter how many faces I stared into none of them would be Lori's. She was gone, her body claimed by the sea. Nothing would change that. I wasn't sure which was worse. Living with the memory of her corpse or living with the lack of resolution. Inventing her face became easier as time went on, as I saw more dead bodies claimed by unforgiving waters. Greater familiarity with her method of death meant cobbling together her final moments and the end result became as routine as signing my name on paperwork.

"Goddamn it, Ellis." He pulled a hand through his thick hair. "What I said to you in Wink—I had no right."

"Survive a loss of that magnitude and then we can talk about acting rationally."

"It's fine." A pleading note entered my voice. "I'll forgive you if you get me out of here."

"Vause will be pissed if she comes looking and can't find you." Mischief glimmered in Graeson's eyes, and I glimpsed the man he had been before losing his sister, who he might be again one day if he fought hard enough. "Come on. Let's go. It's not like she can't find you if she needs to." He traced the bruised skin under my eyes with his finger. "You can catch up on your sleep."

"That sounds…really good." Even better than chai.

"We're having dinner." He helped me stand. "I want you to be awake for it."

"D-dinner," I spluttered. "I didn't agree to—"

"I mentioned you, me and dinner in the same sentence this morning." He took my elbow, and warmth spread from that small contact. "You didn't refuse, which is the same as accepting."

"Why are you doing this?" I tugged against him. "Why do you care?"

"You aren't taking care of yourself," he rumbled. "These girls need you—*I* need you—at your best. If that means force-feeding you and rocking you to sleep at night, I'll do it."

"That won't be necessary." Heat roasted my cheeks until they would have scalded his hands if he touched them again. "I can take care of myself."

"We'll see," he said so dismissively I knew he had already made up his mind to be my keeper for the duration of the case…whether I wanted him to or not.

CHAPTER EIGHT

With two statements due, one on the boy in Wink and one on the interrogation of the girl from Falco, I had spent the last hour curled up in a club chair in my hotel room typing up my mental notes so I could send them to Vause and hopefully avoid another face-to-face meeting with her. The shift into Lori earlier, the sensation of being in her skin, had me avoiding eye contact with myself in reflections. I was too afraid I might glimpse her again, which was the fresh wave of guilt talking, but there you go. Until the old wounds had time to scab, the last thing I wanted was to face the magistrate responsible for picking at them in the first place.

Graeson had been MIA since dropping me off at the hotel. Something about visiting the local wargs. Not that I'd had a lot of time to examine how I felt about his absence since I had tumbled face-first into my bed as soon as I cleared the threshold into my room. Thanks to the power breakfast he fed me, I was upright again four hours later with hangover-like symptoms, but it was a huge improvement over my utter incapacitation in Wink. The big problem now was that my stomach had also woken up, and my dinner date was nowhere to be found. Not that it was a date. I just meant we had plans for dinner. Not plans, but a mutual understanding we would dine together. That sounded official. Like it was business. Like he was hanging around for non-personal reasons, which he was. Right?

Sliding the laptop onto the low coffee table, I stood and stretched my arms over my head. A stack of accordion menus crammed a container by the phone, and I walked over, picking up the two I had skimmed earlier. I didn't have Graeson's cell number, if he carried one, and the phone in his room rang without answer. Harlow wasn't in her room when I checked either, but I got the feeling she was working or else she would have visited. I wasn't worried she might have knocked and I slept through it. She had already proven she had no trouble convincing people to assist her with breaking and entering into places she shouldn't be.

I was deciding between a charbroiled hamburger and pit barbeque when a knock sounded on the door. *Graeson.* A bubble of anticipation rose in my chest. I didn't bother checking the peephole before tugging on the latch. "What sounds better to you? A piggy potato or a fully involved All-American stacker?"

"I'm vegan, actually."

The menu fluttered to the floor. "Oh. Magistrate Vause. Hi."

"May I?" Her gaze tagged the micro seating area opposite my rumpled bed. "We didn't get a chance to speak before you left."

"Sure." Feeling contrite, I nudged the door wider. "Come on in."

One of her guards barged past me and performed a sweep of the area. He reappeared in seconds and all but snapped his heels together. "It's clear."

Magistrate Vause wrinkled her nose but crossed the threshold. The second guard closed the door behind her and, I assume, took point guarding the room from the hall.

"This will have to do." She flicked her wrist toward the pleather sofa. "Fionn?"

The guard swept his fingers through the air and withdrew a packet of moist towelettes from nowhere. Under her watchful eyes, he wiped down the seat, the back and arm. Then he used the same trick to summon a dry cloth to finish the job. Once done he tossed them in the tiny waste bin next to the desk with a wobbly leg. The others were stuffed back into the same invisible seam where he had retrieved them.

"What brings you by so late?" She struck me as the sort to be in her silk pajamas by eight p.m. sharp. I rushed to add, "Not that I mind the visit."

Fake leather creaked when she sat. "I wanted to make sure you were all right." She must have read my doubt. "I also have not received your report on the incident in Wink."

"I'm working on it now." I scooped up the menu before I could step on it and slip. "The day got away from me. I'm on my dinner break."

"Were you expecting someone?"

To lie or tell the truth? "I wanted to touch base with Harlow about her findings."

Vause didn't call me on the lie, but her glossy façade lost a smidgen of its shine. "You've had a very trying day." She picked a speck of lint from her tan pantsuit. "I thought perhaps if we held a discussion here, tonight, that would suffice."

I lowered myself into the chair opposite her as the implication hit me. Vause didn't want a paper trail. Linking me to Wink? Or me to her and her to Wink? Did this have something to do with the Unseelie Magistrate's absence? "All right."

She crossed her legs at the ankles. "Did you manage to complete a classification on the victim?"

"Yes." Remembering the condition of the boy's remains crushed my appetite, making it easier to tuck the menu into the fold between the arm and seat of my chair. "The cause of death was presumed to be drowning, but that's where the similarities ended. The victim's gender and the condition in which the remains were found breaks the pattern." The implication was clear: there had been no reason for me to visit Wink. None at all. "I did manage to inspect the body prior to the attack, and I can confirm he was not one of ours."

"Marshal Thackeray's report mentioned that a man was killed at the scene."

The hallway confrontation between Harlow and Letitia, the marshal's widow, loomed in my mind. "That's what I heard."

Vause resumed her lint-picking with gusto. "What else did you hear?"

A pulse of spellwork set my lips tingling as if I had been sucking on a habanero chili, a reminder to be careful how much I divulged. "Thierry and I mostly talked about our families and how we came to be employed by the conclave."

Vause shifted her weight and crossed her legs, then uncrossed them as though unable to get comfortable on the hard seat. "Thierry could be a valuable asset to you in the future." She caught me watching her squirm and froze. "The circumstances of your meeting were unfortunate, but perhaps the connection will prove fortuitous in time."

Vause was being squirrelier than usual. When magistrates began acting peculiar, bad things happened. Usually to the person who noticed the odd behavior.

Without fanfare, Vause stood, signaling the meeting's end. "I should return to my hotel." Her nose crinkled at the state of my room. "I prefer not to be so…exposed…after dark."

Magistrate sightings were rare outside their respective regions. If someone recognized her, then her Unseelie counterpart would start asking questions I got the feeling Vause didn't want answered. Not yet. Not until she had finished leading me around by the nose.

I gripped the arms of my chair, ready to lever myself to my feet, but she lifted a hand. "I can show myself out." Her gaze lingered on the crumpled menu by my hip. "I understand you left the safe house with the warg today."

"We drove into Falco together."

"Keep an eye on him." She straightened her blouse. "Wargs run hot. We can't risk him damaging this case in the heat of the moment."

Her guard had escorted her into the hallway before I formulated a response. The door shut behind them, and I slumped in my chair, grateful to have avoided butting heads with her over fae law versus native species law for the second time in one day.

My phone rang, but I was out of energy for conversation. I ignored it until the twentieth chime, and yes, I counted, then I accepted the person wasn't giving up until they spoke with me.

"Ellis."

"My, aren't we formal?" Throaty laughter spilled over the line.

"Aunt Dot. Hi." A surge of homesickness swept me upright. "I'm sorry I didn't call sooner."

When I had tried her this morning, I got her answering machine and left a quick message.

"It's all right, pumpkin. I know how you get caught up in your work. Just next time don't leave an old woman waiting on the porch in her jammies. Send one of those email things to Isaac or something."

"I will." I drew my legs into the chair, tucked my knees to my chest and braced to tell her the truth. She would find out eventually—I was a bad liar—and I didn't want to end up with a bar of her homemade soap in my mouth when I fumbled my story. "I overextended on a case. I used too much magic, and it knocked me out for a full day. That's why I missed my flight. It was too late to call when I woke up, so I waited until morning."

Salty curse words peppered her end of the conversation. "Do you need me?"

The question made hot tears burn the backs of my eyes. If I said yes, she would hook her trailer up to her truck, or make Isaac do it, and she would drive straight here without sleeping. For a woman in her early sixties, with no love for technology, she had fully embraced the millennial caffeine culture. I had to pat her down at the grocery store for canned energy drinks and those little bottled shots before we got in the car.

"I'm fine."

"Camille Annalise Ellis, you are never too old for me to bend over my knee. You better be telling me the whole story."

"I am. I promise." I jiggled my wrist so the bracelet Harlow had given me glinted in the low light. "I met someone and—"

"Is he handsome?" she asked coyly.

"No. Well," I amended, "she's pretty, but it's not like that."

"You got me excited there for a minute." Aunt Dot sighed. "I was seeing grandbabies." A considering note entered her voice. "How pretty is this girl you mentioned…?"

"She's a kid, a teenager," I said, exasperated. "She's, I don't know, a friend. I guess."

"You made a friend?" She clapped in the background. "That's wonderful news."

Her wholehearted endorsement of Harlow based on nothing more than the fact she was a warm body willing to befriend me spoke volumes about my social life. Or the sad lack thereof. I'd always had trouble making friends. We traveled so much there wasn't much point in trying. It had been pretty much just me and Isaac growing up, and he got in more fights than I could count once kids realized who I was, what I was. There were no lone Geminis. None. Except me. That made me a freak, and my other cousin, Isaac's twin brother, Theo, was a twerp. Nine times out of ten he was the reason I was outed before the other kids could pinpoint exactly what was wrong about me.

"She kept an eye on me while I recovered." I kicked off my shoes. "Thanks to her—" and the warg I was most definitely not mentioning, "—I'm back at one hundred percent."

"I'm so proud of you," she gushed. "You ought to invite her to come home with you for a visit."

I pinched the bridge of my nose, grateful she couldn't see me. "She's busy with that case I've been working."

"Well, when you two figure out who done it, she'll be ready for a vacation." Aunt Dot was already party-planning in her head. I could tell. "At least ask her, all right?"

"I will," I promised, knowing I would wiggle out of it later with a flimsy excuse.

"When should I expect you home?" The sound of a screen door slamming would have told me she had taken the call outside even if the burst of katydid song hadn't filled the line. "There's no rush, mind you. I'm keeping an eye on your place and keeping your plants watered. I just like to know where my girl is when she isn't home where I can watch after her."

Being called her girl made my chest tighten. She was more of a mother to me than my own had been in the years since Lori died. I didn't know where Mom and Dad were, and I wasn't going to ask. I hadn't seen them in five years and hadn't gotten a card from them in three. Aunt Dot blamed the postal service and us being on the road so often, but we had lived in Three Way for a whole year. I knew the truth, even if she didn't want to accept it or for me to have to face it.

"I should probably let you go." I eyed the clock, and my stomach gurgled. "I'm about to order a late dinner and head to bed."

"You should have eaten hours ago," she chastised. "Maybe you should give me the number for that friend of yours, so I can tell her to keep a closer eye on you."

What Aunt Dot meant was she wanted Harlow's contact information so *she* could keep a closer eye on me.

I crossed my fingers, glad she couldn't see. "I'll think about it."

"Good girl."

I didn't have to fake a yawn to sell how tired I still was. "Night-night."

"Sleep tight," she sang. "Don't let the bedbugs bite."

I ended the call in a much better place than when it started. I even shot off a quick text to Isaac, letting him know I had finally spoken to his mom and that I would update him with my travel itinerary once I had flight times nailed down for my trip home. I didn't wait for a response. He wasn't a text-you-back kind of guy.

I was right back to debating the merits of a late-night burger over a slow-roasted pork sandwich when staccato knocks had me tossing the menu aside for a second time. More cautious now, I approached the door and peeked through the hole. The quick uptick in my pulse at the sight of Graeson drew his attention to the fisheye lens. Coincidence. Had to be. His hearing wasn't that acute. Was it? There was no going back now. I opened the door.

"Graeson." Determination not to be the first one who mentioned food had my fingers tightening on the doorknob. "Did you forget your room number?"

"No." He traced the long groove in the doorframe until he tapped the brassy strike plate with a fingertip. "I remembered yours."

"Nice line." I braced my palm against the doorframe, barring him from entering the room until I decided whether to let him in. "Catch many fish with that one?"

He feigned a wince while rotating his shoulder. "Sorry, old reeling injury. It acts up from time to time."

"You sure are corny for a warg." I peered at him through narrowed eyes. "Are you sure you're not a deer shifter or something? I don't have a salt lick, but I've got a packet of salt in the bottom of my purse. I think. Maybe that was silica."

For a second I thought he would laugh at my weak joke and that maybe I might join in, because I was proud of having made one, but I saw the moment guilt wiped the budding grin from his mouth.

"She would want you to smile." How many times had Aunt Dot used that line on me? Too many. I heard its echo every time I wanted to laugh but didn't. "She wouldn't want you to feel guilty for moving on with your life."

A frown marred his forehead. "Did you move on?"

"I'm still here." Few people outside our breed understood the enormity of that.

"Isn't this the part where you spout more BS about keeping my chin up or something?"

"Would that make you feel better?"

"No."

"Then here's the truth. The condolences get stuck in your head after a while, a string of pep talks and well wishes that loops." My arm dropped. "The phrases don't change. Only the faces of the people saying them do."

"I like you, Ellis." The tightness around his mouth eased. "You're authentic."

"There are worse labels," I joked halfheartedly. "How did your meeting with the local wargs go?"

"As well as can be expected." He shrugged. "Our packs aren't allied. Visiting to pay my respects to their alpha was a formality to preserve the peace. That's all."

I smoothed my expression. "So what brings you by so late?"

"I wanted to ask for your help." The last shreds of possibility that he had just been running late for dinner tore away and fluttered to the carpet where his shifting feet ground my fragile hope to dust. "I think you're the only one who can."

His earnestness plucked at my conscience, and I found myself asking, "What do you need?"

His large body crowded mine, his voice pitched low. "Can we move this somewhere more private?"

I thumped my forehead against the door. It didn't shake loose a new verdict. Apparently I was decided. "Come inside." He shifted his weight, and I noticed the strap of a bag he hadn't had the last time I saw him hooked over one of his shoulders. "What is that?"

He patted the satchel. "Evidence."

What could he have found that I didn't already have access to? And where had he gotten it? Not from unallied wargs, so who? Clearly there were missing links. After all, Vause had sat in this very room and asked me not to file a report on the incident in Wink. I hadn't realized Graeson had those kinds of connections. A shiver skipped down my spine, and I stepped to one side, ushered him inside and turned the lock.

"You brought it with you?" Exasperation trumped my trepidation. "You were that confident I would want to know?"

"You're a mess of conflicting emotions." He tapped his nose. "I can smell it."

"I thought I smelled like grief."

"You do. Sometimes." He slung his bag onto the sofa where Vause had sat and dropped down beside it, nose wrinkling as he inhaled, probably the anti-bac lingering in the air. "But you smell different now than you did when we met. Something is bothering you. It's more than what Vause subjected you to. You're second-guessing yourself. Doubt carries a pungent scent."

"Maybe I am having doubts," I allowed, gesturing toward his satchel. "Does that mean you still want to trust me with this?"

"Yes." No hint of hesitation. "If you didn't question the system when it fails to meet your expectations, then you would either be corrupt or a sheep, and you're neither of those. You care. You proved that in the interrogation room today. Otherwise you sure as hell wouldn't subject yourself to Vause's machinations."

Since I considered myself a decent agent, most days, I didn't disabuse him of the notion. I did plop into the chair across from him while he woke his computer. "Okay." I clasped my hands. "Let me have it."

"I fed the coordinates of each crime scene into an online mapping program." He spun his laptop on his knees so we both had a clear view of the screen. Graeson had made the connection between the crime scenes faster than I had, but he was coming in late and had access to months' worth of intel. "There's a pattern."

"There have been attacks in Arkansas, Missouri, Illinois, Kentucky, North Carolina, South Carolina, Georgia and now Alabama," I agreed, tracing my finger from point to point. "The deaths are occurring clockwise across the map." I tapped the state we both currently occupied. "There is no Alabama victim. Elizabeth McKenna escaped." I slid my finger left. "That means if the conclave wants to get ahead of Charybdis, we have two chances left. We can pick him up here in Falco if he tries again…"

"…or in Mississippi," he finished the thought.

"The question is: what does the pattern mean?" I ran my finger from dot to dot a second time. "I don't know much about spellwork, but that looks like a circle to me, and those are building blocks for all kinds of powerful magic."

"Kelpies *are* magic. They can't practice it. Not like witches and sentient fae do." His gaze went distant. "Animals don't have the same capacity for spellwork as other fae or even mortals."

"So is the shape random, making Charybdis the kelpie?" I tread carefully, fully aware of the prickle in my lips as I skated close to the boundaries of my oath. "Or is the circle intentional, and Charybdis is a fae or witch who's harnessed the beast in order to keep their hands clean?"

One thing was certain. I needed to see the surveillance video Thierry had mentioned, even if I had to fly back to Wink to do it. She was certain a humanoid fae had exited the portal from Faerie, and it had the ability to become intangible. Neither of those things explained how the kelpie got involved. I had to see that tape. I was missing something.

Graeson canted his head, studying me, and I wondered if he scented the spell humming over my skin. "What do you think?"

"The methodology is too precise to be coincidental." I didn't believe it was random animal behavior for a second. "The murders happen like clockwork. I've kept a bag packed by the door because I knew when to expect the call." He encouraged me by leaning forward. "The victims are taken weeks in advance from when their bodies are found. Wink was a mistake. That wasn't his kill. Which means the schedule remained intact until the McKenna girl escaped. He would have taken her—" I battled down nausea, "—and held her captive until it was time to kill her and leave the body where it would be discovered."

"You think he wants the bodies to be found," Graeson mused. "Yet Charybdis chooses secluded areas for his kills."

"The victims could have gone for weeks, maybe months without being discovered. Yet the conclave is right on top of them, almost like they know where he'll strike next." I held up a finger. "Or like he's telling them where to look. He wouldn't be the first serial killer to crave the notoriety. By using remote locations and then tattling to the fae authorities, he would keep humans out of it."

"Assuming he cares about involving humans," he interjected.

Most of Faerie gave about as much consideration to humans as humans did to fleas on a stray cat. Meticulous or not, I doubted Charybdis cared whether mortals or their authorities took notice of his body of work. Based on the assumption he was the fae from the portal, I was betting it was recognition from his own kind that he craved.

"The circle..." His gaze sharpened on the laptop's screen. "Maybe he does need those bodies found. Maybe it's part of the ritual."

The thought had occurred to me, but he seemed more informed in spellwork than I was. "What do you mean?"

"Spells of that scope are often underpinned by sympathetic magic rather than drawing direct from a practitioner. Encircling an entire state is ambitious. Drawing that much power from a single individual would kill them, but Charybdis doesn't shy away from murder." He appeared to ponder that. "Each death might work as an anchor point to the spell. The sacrifice might be enough to nudge the spell into consciousness. It would become self-sustaining. It would feed on the outrage and the anger, even the grief generated from that death by using the site as a focal point."

"The spell would feed itself?" I shivered, and it wasn't because the central air had kicked on in my room. "That means discovery would be a critical point in the process. Perhaps not vanity but necessity." He began massaging his jaw, scratching at his bristles, and I got the feeling he was stalling. "What's wrong?"

A few taps of his fingers zoomed in on the state caught in the middle of the circle. "You've got family in Tennessee, right?"

"Yes." It was a matter of public record, and I had told Harlow, so it wasn't surprising Graeson knew too.

"That doesn't worry you?" He slid his finger along the route of the crime scenes, like a secondary pattern might emerge if he retraced the path often enough. "Once that circle is completed, it will enclose your home state."

"I'm keeping an eye on it," I assured him. "Right now we have no reason to believe the residents are in any danger."

Setting the circle was ambitious, sure, and creating a magical anchor that was self-sustaining was mind-boggling, yes, but closing a spell that enormous? It would require a level of power unseen in this realm. Until we had reason to believe it could be done, asking my family to vacate their home of the past twelve months felt premature. Isaac wouldn't mind, and Aunt Dot was itching to buy into a new zip code, but I kept dragging my heels. Requesting a new assignment wasn't the issue. The Earthen Conclave couldn't deny me because Gemini were drifters by nature, and they were all about accommodating the inherent needs of the fae species in their employ. What bogged me down was the unexpected pleasure I got from always knowing where to book my flights, always knowing where to go when a job ended. Putting in for a transfer meant packing up and moving. Again. It meant leaving behind all the good memories attached to our current location.

Three Way was starting to feel like more than a pad of concrete where I parked my trailer. It almost felt like…home.

Graeson grunted, drawing my attention back to him. "How do you know so much about spellwork?"

"My brother-in-law's a witch." A few taps on his phone's screen pulled up an image of a slender man with tan skin and black hair wearing a bored expression standing with his legs spread and arms held out to his sides. Children dangled from each of his limbs as though he were a living jungle gym. A curvy woman with the same hazel eyes as Graeson stood in the background. She covered her mouth while she laughed. "His opinions can't be included in any official record since the conclave most likely wouldn't hire him, even as a consultant, because of his pack affiliation, but he's a coven leader. The man knows his magic. He's volunteered to help with what comes next."

"What's that exactly?" I asked hesitantly.

"You lied to me and to Marshal Comeaux," he said casually, as though he hadn't just been inquiring about my family. The accusation punched me in the gut. I didn't see it coming. I should have. I knew he hadn't forgiven or forgotten that small fact. "You touched Marie." A few more clicks. "I saw what you did with the McKenna girl. You knew her species after holding her hand." He glanced up, and our eyes met. "What else can you tell?"

My lips compressed into a stubborn line. When he said he had evidence to gain entrance to my room, I hadn't realized he meant against *me*.

"Conclave purse strings are tight from what I hear." *Click. Click. Click.* Thick fingers punished the keyboard. "The only way the conclave is footing the bill to fly you around the country for this case instead of hiring local talent is if you're providing a service no one else can. At least not all in one package."

"Classification is a rare talent."

"That's not the service I mean."

The blood rushed from my face and left my lips as cold as the underbelly of a glacier. The backs of my knees hit the edge of the chair and buckled. I sat down hard and couldn't get my feet under me even though I wanted to put as much distance as possible between us. "You mean Lori."

His absence suddenly made a lot more sense. While I was napping, he must have been doing his research, plotting the second he understood the breadth of my talent. His eagerness to use me shouldn't have stung. He had all but told me at breakfast he was tending what he saw as an asset. Lucky him, his short-term investment had paid off the second I walked into that interrogation room.

"We're tracking a fae who's murdering children." He made it sound as if it was his case, like he was doing me a favor by explaining things. "This possibility must have crossed your mind."

"No." I gripped the armrests and sank my nails into the pleather. "I can honestly say the thought of using my dead sister as bait to catch a serial killer never crossed my mind. Not even once."

I spent hours a day careful *not* to think about her, so no, even as freely as I offered my other services, I had never considered using Lori. Not once. Not ever. She was a private torment made public by necessity, and that was my mistake. "I'm not some menu you can order services from." Rage trembled in my fingers. "Magistrate Vause—"

"Don't try to defend her." Gold devoured his irises until his eyes were shimmering pools of gilded rage. "I stood right beside her in that blacked-out room and watched the fucked-up show she orchestrated." A snarl entered his voice. "What she did to you was cruel, and do you know how she felt when you walked into the room? *Smug*." The laptop made a popping sound where his fingers dented the plastic. "She sprang it on you without warning because she knew you would balk, she knew you would never consider using that gift yourself, and she exploited your pain. You were suffering in front of an audience while she patted herself on the back at a job well done."

"Magistrates are sidhe nobles. They come from power and influence, and they're ruthless." Anyone who had crossed one wore the scars. I had several myself. "Vause isn't going to offer me a teddy bear or a plate of fried potatoes for doing what she views as my job, and I don't expect her to."

"Then why do you smell so wounded?" His gaze cooled until his eyes were hazel once again. "Are you hurt because I pulled the blinders off your eyes?"

My thoughts were a runaway train of regret. *I wanted you to be different. I wanted an uncomplicated meal with a handsome guy without an agenda. I wanted you to like me for me, not for what I can do for you.* I had been a fool to forget, even for a second, that he entered my life when Marie exited his. Her passing linked us, not a mutual like or respect, but a job. One he expected me to do no matter the cost. I didn't know how to put any of that into words, so I didn't try. "I think you should leave."

"No."

"*No?*" I gritted my teeth. "This is my room. You don't get to make that call."

"I'm the only person in this game who won't lie to you, Ellis. I'm not sneaking around behind your back. I'm not lying to you or trying to trick you." His earnest expression never wavered. "I'm sitting right here in front of you, laying all my cards on the table. I'm being honest." His jaw flexed. "I want to use you—as Lori—for bait. Together I think we can end this."

Laughter sliced up the back of my throat. "Hypocrite much?"

"I never said Vause had a bad idea." He looked pained to give her that much credit. "Manipulation isn't the right way to go about asking for your help. She shouldn't have kept Lori in her back pocket like an ace in the hole in the event the conclave managed to corral Charybdis and needed an operative to bring him down. The day she pulled your file and chose you for this was the day she should have confronted you with her plan. That's what I believe, and my being here ought to be proof of that." His shoulders tensed. "I've told you what I need from you. Will you help me?"

The question lingered between us, and I sat there rubbing at a grease stain on my knee from the bacon I had eaten at the breakfast we had shared this morning, the one where I thought tonight would be ending with a belly full of food and not rage. I embraced the anger. It broiled away my aching uncertainty into a flawless clarity that allowed me to appreciate what he was saying, the logic of it, and then wield that same instrument to deduce what he wasn't.

"You weren't surprised." The truth slammed into me. "In Falco, you weren't surprised I could shift." Most folks were stunned where he had been sympathetic. It wasn't a talent I often showcased for good reason, yet he took it all in stride. A worse possibility dawned. "Were you at the Wink Sinks? Is that how you knew?"

"I interviewed one of the marshals." Tension in the air thickened, and he admitted, "He told me what you did."

So he had come to find me knowing I could shift even if he hadn't grasped the parameters of my abilities.

"That explains the white-glove service." Feeding me, driving me around and hauling my luggage up to my room. "You wanted to keep an eye on me until you figured out what Vause saw in me." I felt sick. Nauseous. I wanted to crawl in bed, pull the covers over my head and stay there for a month. "Then you saw Lori, and the cogs started turning."

"The killer is targeting young fae girls," he pressed. "Tell me it's a coincidence you can shift into a child's form. Not an illusion, an actual child. Tell me Vause doesn't know exactly how to play on your guilt over Lori to coerce you into doing what I'm asking you to do of your own free will."

I got to my feet and smoothed the wrinkles from my pants.

"Where are you going?" he demanded.

"You won't leave my room, so I'll go." I walked to the door and snagged my purse too fast for him to dump the contents off his lap and come after me. "Make sure you lock up when you're done."

Once out in the hall, I made the short trip to Harlow's room. The "Do Not Disturb" sign still hung from the lever. So much for hiding out with her. There went my buffer. I pulled out my phone and dialed her number but got punted straight to voicemail.

The late hour and the warg occupying my room left me with few options. Figuring Harlow must still be on the scene in Falco, I rode the elevator down to the lobby and called a cab. Cellphones and water didn't mix, so it made sense she wouldn't keep hers on her. I'd head out there, give myself time to cool off, and she could give me a ride back to the hotel. I would treat her at one of those twenty-four-hour restaurants that did brisk business preying on interstate traffic with their glossy signs and promises of bottomless mugs of coffee. Right now that kind of anonymity hit the spot.

CHAPTER NINE

Brushy Creek Lake resembled all the other lake turned crime scenes I had visited since Charybdis began his murder spree. He definitely had a preference for the remote and the tick-infested.

"You sure you don't want me to hang around?" The cabbie leaned out his window, scratching his cheek as he took in the desolate location. A full moon hung overhead, muted by the thick beams of his headlights. "I got a daughter your age. I wouldn't leave her out here's all I'm sayin'."

"You don't have to worry about me." I pointed to the far end of the weedy parking lot where a black van straddled crumbling white lines. "That's my ride home. I'm meeting a friend here."

"Friend? Hope you don't mean a guy. Only one thing they want if they ask you to meet them at a van in the woods." He huffed. "It ain't right. No *friend* of yours ought to drag you out here in the middle of the damn night."

Smothering a grin at the human working himself into a protective frenzy over me, I took pity on his conscience and removed my ID from the purse slung over my shoulder. I flipped open the wallet and presented my badge, which was enchanted to appear to him as what he expected to see, whether that meant local law enforcement or a government agency. Still wary, he pulled a flashlight out of his console and swept it down the side of the van, illuminating the seal of the local marshal's office, which was also glamoured to meet his expectations.

"I guess you can take care of yourself, huh?" He squinted at the badge one last time. "You keep my number, all right? I'm on the clock until six this morning. If you run into any trouble, you give me a call."

"I will," I promised, stepping back to give him room to execute a three-point turn.

His hand twisted in a slight wave, and he was gone.

Night sounds creeped over me as I stood, allowing my eyes to adjust to the gloom. That the noise and light from the cab hadn't brought Harlow running wasn't a great sign. I crossed to the van and found it empty, as expected. I checked the handle. The door was unlocked. I used the step and braced a knee on the front seat to get a look around. A pair of lime-green skate shoes sat on the front passenger seat, but her cellphone was nowhere in sight. I peered into the night through the windshield.

"You shouldn't be out here alone."

My head popped up and smacked the ceiling of the van. Rubbing the sore spot, I climbed out and slammed the door hard enough the vehicle rocked. Graeson stood cloaked in shadow.

"What's wrong?" I grimaced. "Afraid Charybdis might nab me before you get the chance to toss me at him?"

Graeson stepped from the trees into the parking lot, and moonlight kissed his bare skin. He was naked. Fully nude. Not a scrap of clothes on him. I'm not proud of how long I struggled to drag my focus from his navel to his gaze. A few inches lower, and I would never be able to make eye contact with the man again.

"My plan involves a team operating in a controlled environment where you're kept perfectly safe, not rushing into the unknown without backup." Another step closer. "I would never allow you to be harmed. Not even to capture him."

Except he already had, whether he knew it or not, by pretending to be interested when all the while he was sizing me up for other reasons.

"You seem to have lost your clothes," I pointed out, voice higher than usual.

"I heard you tell the cabbie where to take you. I shifted and followed. It was fastest." He frowned at his body, as if not seeing the problem. "It's too dangerous for you to be out here alone."

"I'm not alone." My traitorous gaze dipped to his collarbone before I caught it sliding south and jerked it up to his jawline. "Harlow is out here somewhere. Her belongings are still in this van."

He tipped his face into the wind. “All the scents here are hours old.”

“Then where is she?” I turned back to the van. “Her shoes are in there. She can’t have gone far without them.”

“You’re assuming she was on two legs. She is a mermaid…sometimes.” He hesitated as if her dual nature confused him too. “She might still be in the water.”

Foreboding slithered down my spine. “Her team wouldn’t have left if she was MIA.”

“Are you sure?” His tone made it clear he figured the marshals for deserters.

The urge to defend the conclave parted my lips, but I had seen how the marshals in Wink treated Harlow, and that was before she got one of their own killed. Gossip spread fast among fae. Soon it would be hard for her to find work, and walking onto a job would mean watching her back. She had faced this new team and new location alone, and I got a bad feeling about that.

I picked a direction and launched my one-woman search party. “I’m going to look for her.”

“I’ve scented Harlow and the McKenna girl,” he called. “I’ll be able to track down where the attack happened.”

I kept walking.

“The lake is in the other direction,” he yelled helpfully.

I let my head fall back until the sky filled my vision. When no divine help was forthcoming, I straightened my shoulders and faced the naked man. My eyes wanted to map his body in search of more tattooed skin when I should have wanted to parade him through the brush in the hopes his free-range trouser-snake got snagged by briars or brushed against poison ivy.

“Let’s get this over with,” I huffed.

He chuckled under his breath. “There’s the spirit.”

He set off in the opposite direction, leaving me with a prime view of his muscled shoulders and a different kind of full moon shining below his waist. I didn’t look. For long. Nice butt or not, he and I wanted different things from each other. Not that I wanted him. I mean, I barely knew him, but he was easy on the eyes, and I hadn’t seen a naked man in…

“Watch your step.”

My head jerked up, but I stumbled over the knotted clump of vines anyway and fell against Graeson's chest when he turned to catch me. Our forearms locked together while he fought to keep me from face-planting, and I recoiled to avoid touching more of his sweaty, muscled skin than necessary. I ended up smashed between him and a tree with him gripping my wrists at shoulder height, both of us breathing hard and fast.

"You can release me now." Being pinned against the trunk by a naked warg seemed like a dangerous place to be. "Any day now."

The warg gazed down at me with expectation that made my cheeks burn, but he let me go, and we resumed our hike into the marsh. It took a while for us to reach the darkly glittering body of water where the kelpie had hunted the McKenna girl, and Graeson ended up steadying my elbow when my feet bogged in mud more than once, though we managed to avoid another tree incident. I didn't thank him. I shrugged him off and trudged on, looking for an indication of where Harlow had gone into the water, but the sand hadn't been disturbed by a sometimes-mermaid. All I had to tell me we were on the right track was Graeson's nose, and that seemed more interested in sniffing me than the ground.

"Why don't we split up?" I suggested. "You can search by scent, over there near the water, and I'll head deeper into the woods."

Farther away from you was implied.

"No." He didn't entertain the thought longer than it took to shoot down my idea. "We stick together. There's something off about this place." He stopped to rub a leaf through his fingers then sniffed them. "We know Charybdis was here, so was the McKenna girl, so were the chaperones who answered her cries for help and the search crew the conclave dispatched, and so was Harlow." He stepped forward and repeated the process. "Yet I haven't picked up a single scent that isn't coming from you or me since we left the area surrounding the van."

"Could it be an erasure spell?" Fae scents often frightened local wildlife. Several fae species were custodians of the earth, and they advocated such measures in order to do no harm to the animals. Erasure spells created sensation voids, which spooked animals too, but not as much as the predator smells did. Over time, after a good rain, the antiseptic magic washed away to be replaced with more natural aromas. "Can you tell if it's charm based?"

"They're too good for that. The absence is telling, though. I don't like this. Someone wiped the entire lakefront. That shouldn't have happened until all support personnel had cleared the area." Pointing to the deer trail I had been following, he ordered, "Stay close. I'm going to try tracking by the water."

Magic and water didn't mix. If we had walked into an enchantment, wading into the water might break it. I was fine letting him play the guinea pig. I preferred being head blind to waterlogged.

Graeson kept to the sandbars as we circled the perimeter of the lake while I traversed the solid ground, walking beside him but six or seven feet away from even the barest hint of moisture. Every so often, I caught his head tilting back, tracking our progress by the moon.

"Is it true what they say about wargs?" I peered through the canopy of pine needles overhead. "Can you only change during full moons?"

"That's personal." He seemed to consider it a moment. "But I owe you one, so I'll answer." We walked in silence for a few minutes. "The more dominant the wolf, the easier the moon's song is to ignore. New wolves get moonsick and fly into rages. Older wolves have better control. Some wolves—" he cut his eyes toward me, "—don't need the moon to change at all."

Trees flashed between us as I kept pace with him, and each flicker revealed a subtle shift in his expression. "What does it feel like when you change?"

A hitch in his stride was the only indication I had struck a nerve. "How does it feel when *you* change?"

The bite of his words stung, but only a little. I had expected him to lash out, maybe even wanted his irritation to clash with mine. It felt more authentic than his oh-so-helpful facade. "It feels like being turned inside out." I waited for the lump in my throat to subside. "It's worse for me because Lori is much smaller than I am now. It's a lot of Camille to cram into such a tight space."

Had I glimpsed pity in his gaze, I might have spun around and marched back to the car, Harlow be damned. His eyes held only moonlight, and to my surprise, he answered a second question.

"Every bone breaks. Skin tears. Ligaments are shredded." He leapt from one sandbar to the next. "You want to know the worst part? It's the fur. Most folks think it's the bones, but hell, kids break bones." Though not on the scale he endured. "Having thousands of thick strands of fur pierce through your skin like needles through cloth? Now that *hurts*."

A shudder rippled through my shoulders. "Okay, you win."

"It's not a contest." He shot me a halfhearted smile. "Physical pain can be overcome with enough practice. There are worse ways to ache."

I let my silence stand for agreement. "Are you picking up on anything yet?"

"There are multiple scent layers. Humans mostly. A few dogs." He rubbed his nose as though to rid himself of a tickle. "Those smells are old. Nothing fae yet."

We must have circled almost back to where we started when I shoved through a dense layer of brush, and my next footstep sank into powdery sand, the kind trucked in to create manmade beaches. "It looks like we're headed into a picnic area."

Graeson didn't respond. The warg was nowhere in sight.

I shoved aside a tangle of thorny smilax vine and found him squatting over an indentation in the sand. "Graeson?"

"It was here," he growled, fingers piercing the grains to produce a luminescent scale he held aloft, one too large to have come from a mermaid of Harlow's stature. He stood in a fluid motion and vanished in a blur of flexing muscle.

The calm waters mocked me. A jump down to the sandbar would save me time chasing him, but I couldn't do it. Instead I turned on my heel and bolted for the picnic area. Splashing noises interrupted the still night. I followed the ruckus, keeping a few yards between me and the edge of the lake.

I stepped on a pinecone camouflaged by decaying leaves and rolled my ankle. My back hit a nearby tree, but this time there was no one to catch me. I grunted on impact and leaned against the trunk, shifting the weight off that foot. I lifted my leg to inspect it, and the ground roiled under my heel. More pinecones emerged from the detritus, shaking off their spiny backs while marching toward me, circling me.

"What the—?"

Tiny eyes gleamed in the faint light. For the love of pancakes. Those weren't pinecones. They were igel, and the twerps had learned from our run-in in Wink. This time they hadn't come alone. Two dark shapes glided forward. Only the glittering rims of their outlines gave them away. *Umbras*. Shadow servants. Light bent around the figures, blurring their features into masklike smoothness.

A throaty howl raised gooseflesh down my arms.

Graeson.

"Can we talk about this?" I asked the nearest *umbra*. He rustled a response that probably meant *no*, because he swung a long arm at my head. I ducked then popped up kissing-close to its maw. "Graeson?" I shrilled. "Feel free to jump in at any time."

One of the shapes peeled away from the other and drifted into the shadows. Great. I had set him on the warg's trail.

I struck out, but my fist shot through the smoky creature. Perfect. It was going to be one of those nights. The billowing mass inched forward. I backed up a step, stumbled on an igel that was quick to burrow under my heel, and lost balance. The blackness enveloped one of my flailing arms in a chilling embrace and hauled me closer.

Snarls rippled over the water. Limbs snapped and leaves rustled as the second shadow located its prey. A yelp sounded, and the creature billowed toward me with a silver and white wolf writhing in its stomach.

"Graeson," I breathed, and his golden eyes lifted to mine.

"Tonight just keeps getting better," a sultry voice announced. "Who have we got here?"

The angry woman I recognized from the hotel hallway in Wink, the widow who had jumped Harlow, stepped into a beam of moonlight. I had been wrong. She wasn't just angry. She was so far beyond pissed there wasn't a word for her volatile state. Violent energy radiated from her, and my pulse galloped once she got near enough for the tendrils of her insidious powers to caress me.

"She's not an igel." I had no idea if the wolf understood me, but I had to warn him. "She's a Fury."

Her nearness suffocated. Foam slid past my lips, down my chin. I vibrated with so much rage, my eyes rolled back in my head. Dragging myself out from under that torrent left me sweating.

"You came to find the mermaid." Her black gaze burned through me. Her big toes dragged twin trails through the sand, but her feet no longer touched the ground. "You're the one who left the messages on her phone."

Well that explained why Harlow had been out of contact. "Where is she?"

"You should leave," she told the slavering wolf. "I have no quarrel with you or yours."

"She…is…*mine*."

The sound of Graeson's rasping voice snapped my head toward him. Suspended inside the shadow's gut, he had managed a partial shift without drawing our attention. Sweat beaded his skin, and his bones glided under his muscles, distorting his proportions from that of a wolf into a man.

"Is that true?" The shadow holding me squeezed as Letitia considered me. "Do you belong to the wolf?"

Accepting his claim stamped my ticket out of danger, but Harlow wouldn't be as lucky. She had screwed up in Wink, and if found guilty, she would be punished for her actions, but it wasn't up to the grief-ravaged Fury to decide her fate. That's what magistrates were for. We had a justice system for a reason.

"What happened in Wink was my doing." I lifted my chin. "Harlow was struggling, and I rushed in to help. The others followed my lead. Your husband's death was my fault. Not hers."

"Ellis," Graeson snarled through his contorted jaw. "Don't be…a hero."

Ignoring the warg was easy with a pissed-off Fury breathing hatred in my face. *"You."* It was the only word she managed to get past her trembling lips. She made it sound like the worst insult imaginable. "Bring her." The shadow holding me bobbed in her wake, riding the heat waves streaming from her skin like a hawk soaring on a thermal updraft.

"Ellis."

"Kill the wolf. I can't risk him or his pack coming after her." The Fury appreciated the glistening water. "Drown him in the lake and leave him there. Let the creature finish him off."

The shadow rippled then stuffed a smoky hand down the wolf's throat to quiet him.

"The kelpie?" I struggled against my captor. "You saw it?"

"It drove the mermaid from the lake." She pointed to the spot where Graeson had burst into a ball of fur. "She was flopping on the shore. All I had to do was scoop her up."

Flopping meant Harlow had been wearing her fins. Why this time? What made her change for this dive? In order to beach herself, she had been in mermaid mode when she confronted the kelpie. At least this confirmed she had survived the encounter.

"Was anyone else out here?" I swiped my arms through my wispy captor while getting my feet under me. "Did you see anyone with the kelpie?"

"A small girl," she said in a somber voice. "I sent the *umbra* to check. She was already dead. I couldn't help her."

My eyes crushed shut. That meant Charybdis had claimed its victim in this state after all.

That hairline crack in the Fury's armor compelled me to add, "If you don't release me, other girls like her will die."

"Girls like her will grow up without a father thanks to you and your friend." Her earlier anger expanded tenfold. "You're expendable. That's what the conclave taught me with Jasper's death. You're all disposable. You and your friend will die for your crimes, and others will take your place. You'll be reduced to a name on a memorial wall that your coworkers walk past, seeing but not *seeing*."

Vicious snapping noises preceded the splashing of water. No matter how Graeson fought, he was hauled into the lake by the second shadow as sure as if he were captured in a silver mesh net.

"Let him go." I screamed my frustration. "He wasn't in Wink. He has nothing to do with this."

"He cares about you," she seethed, "and that's reason enough for him to die."

Telling her I barely knew Graeson—or Harlow—wouldn't save them. Letitia existed in a space beyond reality, beyond rationality, where vengeance and pain were the only flavors she tasted and blood was the only way to erase the cosmic debt she had attached to Harlow, and now to me.

"Keep her quiet," the Fury ordered my personal *umbra*. "She might have brought more agents with her. We'll have to handle those too."

A chill embraced me. "Where are the other marshals?"

"Where all good marshals go when they die," she said coldly and turned her back on me. "Come, pets. Let's go home."

The shadow crammed its wispy fist down my throat until I gagged. I bit down, tasting air. The creature had no blood to draw, no skin to read. I had nothing to mimic. My talents were useless against it.

A gurgled yelp fueled my thrashing. The creature clamped down harder, crushing me in its embrace. Wet snarls were the last thing I heard before the shadow squeezed out my consciousness.

CHAPTER TEN

I woke with the earthy taste of mold in the back of my throat and a stiff lower back. I pushed myself upright off the poured concrete slab floor that radiated with cold and stank of mildew. Cinder-block walls supported the unfinished ceiling over my head. Pipes and wires hung exposed and within easy reach. I briefly wondered how the *umbras* might like the taste of electricity before deciding I was as likely to fry my brain as theirs and dismissed the idea as more dangerous than my current circumstances. At least for now.

Rolling onto my feet and shaking out my tingling limbs, I made a quick visual sweep of the room. No window. One door missing its knob. A fist-sized hole had been punched through the plaster beside it so that a chain could be looped through the circular cutout and locked on the opposite side. No handy tools had been left out so I could pick the lock, or lever against the chain to snap it. No food or water or blankets. Scrape together everything in what appeared to be a basement cell, and I had a whole lot of nothing.

Disjointed memories of my abduction sank back into my skull in bits and pieces.

The grieving widow. The shadow creatures. Those damn igel.

And Graeson.

He couldn't be dead. He was a warg, practically bulletproof unless the rounds were silver.

I picked crusted saliva off my chin and out of the corners of my mouth while listening for signs of life. Worst-case scenario, I had been crammed into a storm shelter or detached cellar of some kind. Best-case scenario, I was holed up in the basement of the Rebec family home. Letitia had said *Let's go home* after all. Neither option gave me the warm fuzzies.

As my eyes adjusted, I distinguished a set of figures drawn on the wall in sweeping pink and blue lines. Sidewalk chalk. A booming noise startled me, and I crept to the door and peered through the hole. Cases of soda were stacked against the wall near what might have been a set of stairs. Beside those a washing machine hopped as it struggled with its load. It jumped hard to the right, and a basket filled with equal part toys and laundry spilled onto the floor. *Rebec house it is.*

If I was here, then where was Harlow? And if this was the Rebec home, then was *here* in Wink, Texas?

Air whistled through the crack where my eye had been, and I recoiled as the room filled with familiar dense smog. I didn't waste time swatting at it this time. I let it coalesce undisturbed, and as I watched, two silver gashes that must have been eyes blinked open. The *umbra* appraised me through the churning blackness with suspicion, confirming my fears that it was far more sentient than I first thought.

"Where's the mermaid?" I demanded.

Spears of white light flashed in a skeleton grin.

Is Graeson alive? That was the question I meant to ask next, but the words stuck in my throat. Graeson and I weren't friends. He'd wrecked that possibility when he decided to use me. But I didn't want him dead. We had gazed into the barren craters where our chest cavities ought to be and *known* one another, and I didn't want to be alone in my grief again so soon.

The creature fluttered on my periphery, waiting, its ominous fingers unfurling through my hair. I stood unmoved, challenging it. "Where is Mrs. Rebec?"

Its fleeting amusement snuffed in a blink, and the eyes vanished along with the rest of its expression.

Metal scraped. I whirled as the door opened, and the man from the hotel hallway entered the room. If memory served, he was Letitia's brother. He also appeared to be catnip to the umbra, who vibrated with pleasure at the sight of him, curling around the man's torso like an inner tube made of smoke. He patted it absently as he appraised me through muddy-brown eyes puffed from lack of sleep. A plain white T-shirt was tucked into his jeans. Boots crusted with muck left prints behind him. His appearance was as bland as the dirt-colored hair on top of his head.

"Where is Harlow?" The unanswered question thing was getting old.

"She's been taken to the gully." The man hooked his thumbs over the *umbra* and slid it down to the floor, where he stepped out of it. The shadow puddled forlornly across the concrete, spilling long across the cement until he approximated the man's shape. "Letitia asked me to bring you," he said to me. "You can walk, or I can have you carried."

Whatever the gully was, he made it sound like the last place he wanted to go, which couldn't bode well for Harlow or for me. I shifted forward a fraction, until my shadow overlapped the *umbra*. It peeled off the floor and rose in a vaporous column that drifted between me and the man, who cast no shadow at all. That explained how Letitia came by at least one of her servants. "You can't let her do this."

"I can't stop her." He massaged his swollen eyes with his fingertips. "No one can. She's a Fury. She won't be sane again until her thirst for vengeance is sated."

"She's going to kill me and the mermaid. Do you want our deaths on your conscience?" I waited for a flicker of pity, something. I got nothing. He was empty. Drained. Furies burned out everyone around them, and this guy was crispy. "I'm an agent with the Earthen Conclave. When this is over, you're going to prison for a very long time."

His lips parted and then closed. When he exited the room, steps that had trudged earlier seemed lighter somehow.

I followed without him prompting me, closing the gap between us with long strides that made my calves burn. All the while his shadow breathed ice on my nape. One step closer. Two. By the third I could have reached out and tapped him on the shoulder. I lunged, smashing against an invisible barrier that rattled my brain, and I slid to the floor in a daze.

A witch. The man was a witch. I hadn't touched him, but I read his magic easily.

The man didn't break stride as he motioned to the *umbra*. Eager to please its master, the shadow consumed me. The now familiar chittering noises announced the arrival of the igel. A sea of tiny bodies made for an undulating carpet of spines, and the shadow laid me to rest on top of them. I hissed through my teeth as their needles pierced the sensitive flesh on my skull, back, hips and calves. Once skewered properly, I bit back a whimper as hundreds of dainty feet scrabbled across the grimy linoleum, causing the spines to shift—and my skin to tear—with them.

Somehow the little beasts scuttled up the stairs and out of the house while supporting my weight. Night had fallen during my captivity. From my new position, inches from the ground and flat on my back, the sky hung infinite and solemn above me.

Gemini derived their name from the Zodiac. The story goes that Castor and Pollux were twin brothers known as the Dioskouri. Castor was the son of Tyndareus, the king of Sparta, and a mortal. Pollux was the son of Zeus, and a demigod. Their mother was Leda. To make a Greek tragedy short, Castor was killed. In his grief, Pollux asked that his father allow him to share his immortality with his twin so they could remain together. Zeus agreed, and they were transformed into the constellation Gemini.

That said, I couldn't point out our namesake constellation if my life depended on it.

Bright stars glittered above me, and they were nameless and heartless as they watched my progress.

Locked in the shadow's chill embrace, I conserved my energy and strained my ears for hints about what came next. Never in my wildest dreams did I expect to hear cheering and whistling coming from behind me, in the direction the hedgies were hustling.

The noise grew deafening as we pierced a ring of light that washed yellow and warm over my eyes. Smoke stung my nostrils. A waft of burnt citronella made my eyes sting. Toenails clicked on a smooth surface, and the convoy ground to a halt. The gully, it turned out, was a deep wash behind a sprawling clapboard house. The igel mucked through a bed of smoothed clay the pale gray of Unseelie skin. Faces ringed the crumbling ledges above, peering down at me. Money exchanged hands. Popcorn—seriously?—rained over my head. The firelight illuminated the area where I was being held but left the spectators their anonymity. Still, I had a good guess as to who they were.

Furies were rare. At least as rare as Geminis. They were usually born into witch families, making them one of the few fae who sprung from humans. Except not really. A Fury's soul was immortal. Its flesh was temporary housing. What that meant in most cases was a Fury latched on to a human early in its life, kicked its soul to the curb and became the person. It would live that life, procreating like mad, until its body grew old and died, and then it would leap into the next suitable vessel in its lineage and begin again.

So if I had to guess who—other than Jasper's igel family—would be so eager to watch the show, I would place my bets on Letitia's coven, of which her mother and brother must also be members.

Footsteps padded toward me. An old woman, who I recognized as the final member of the trio who'd confronted Harlow in Wink, leaned over me, tight-lipped and indifferent. She pointed a gnarled finger to the left, and the shadow wrenched my neck so I had to look or my head would pop off.

Harlow hung suspended by the second *umbra*. Her feet were bare and her legs smooth. The tail was gone again. Microscopic denim shorts rode low on her hips. A swath of pale skin glowed warm in the torchlight between the waistband and the hem of her neoprene top.

"Release me." Though my head was still cranked to one side, I cut my eyes to their corners to glare up at the old woman. "She's made no secret she plans to kill us. The only way we all walk away from this is if you release me and the mermaid. Now."

Her puckered lips plumped as she considered my demand. "I will no' cross that girl, child, lest I surrender me own life in place of yours." She bared bright pink gums. "I'm old, but I'm no' dead yet."

"Gazing through the bars of a prison cell is not how I would choose to end my life," I threatened.

She leaned over, nudging me with her toe, and a pentacle necklace slid from the deep collar of her blouse. "Who do ye think ye are to threaten me?"

Playing off a hunch, I spelled it out for her. "I'm an agent with the Earthen Conclave. I've been to the Crathie Prison, where all the convicted earth witches are sent to die, and I can tell you it's a special kind of hell tailored to the needs of its prisoners." She fisted the pentacle for strength, and I knew I had her. Magic was passed down the maternal lines. The man was a witch, and so she must be too. "You will never again feel rain on your skin, dirt in your hands or nurse tender shoots to maturity. Your connection with the earth will be severed, and you will die surrounded by concrete and steel."

Pursed lips moved in a circular motion. *"I want immunity for meself and me boy. Goddess knows he has suffered enough."*

I jumped at the sound of her voice. I hadn't expected to hear it inside my head. The privacy was welcome, though. "Give me a hand—" and I meant that literally, "—and I promise you and your son full immunity."

"Shadow and light canno' exist in ta same place at ta same time."

"Wait." I writhed. *"That can't be it. What does it mean?"*

"Figure it out." She thumped my temple with her knuckle. *"I canno' do all the work for ye."*

A riddle. Great. They might as well shoot me now.

After giving me a decisive nod, she toddled out of my line of sight. Only then did I notice despite the firelight, she cast no shadow. Letitia had enslaved hers too. I could guess where it had gone. It must be the one confining Harlow. I wondered which had dragged Graeson into the lake, but remembering his ear-piercing howls made my chest hurt, so I focused on what the old woman said, hoping that scrap of insight might save Harlow and me.

"Bring her," Letitia keened in a high voice that shattered my train of thought. "Let all witness justice for my Jasper."

The shadow hefted me upright, and my head spun as the blood rushed back to my brain. "Oh fudge."

A beer bottle thudded beside my foot, and a booming voice yelled, "Are we doing this or what?"

Apparently the natives were getting restless.

Letitia gestured me forward, and I had no choice about going. The nearer I came to her, the hotter my skin burned, the harder my gut twisted. Her black gaze pierced the depths of my soul and ignited the petty, squabbling tangle of faded emotional baggage we all carry until each of those old hurts smoldered with renewed fervor.

She leaned in, and her lips brushed my cheek. Rage boiled in the kiss, and it scalded my mind until the wisps of my thoughts evaporated. There was nothing. *I* was nothing. All that remained was Letitia. Her will. Her power. I understood now. I understood *everything.*

The mermaid had to die.

She pointed a finger at a woman with delicate features and pastel hair. She had slender legs, not fins, but Letitia was insistent. "Kill her. Kill the mermaid."

I didn't think. I didn't question. I ran at the slumped figure. A shadow kept pace with me, its insidious whispers stoking the ravenous fire smoldering within me. Fingers curled into claws, I swiped at the woman's face with my blunt fingernails. She brought her arm up and blocked me, our elbows tangling, and that rush of contact sent a haze of cool magic flowing up my arm.

Gentle energy crackled over my skin, and the Fury's blinding haze cleared. *Harlow*. Fresh horror seized my heart as her magical signature registered.

There was none.

Harlow was…human.

"Run," I rasped.

"I can't." An *umbra* pooled around her ankles, cementing her to the spot. "It's all right, Cam."

No. This was all kinds of not right. The contact magic was fading, and my memories dulled with it.

Who was this girl? Why had I attacked her? What about her made me so angry?

"What is this?" Letitia shrieked. "I told you to kill her."

Each stomp of her foot as she approached ground my awareness under her heel. Fighting the compulsion left me trembling and weak with sweat pouring down my forehead into my eyes.

"Tell my folks I would have come home. Can you do that for me?" Harlow's voice trembled. "Tell them I would have chosen the Mother."

The Mother. She meant the ocean. She would have returned home to her pod at the end of her year. What kind of human claimed merfolk as kin? What sort of mortal called the sea home? If Letitia had her way, I would never learn the truth of the peculiar little un-mermaid.

I captured her hand between my damp ones. *"Please."*

Unsure which of us I was begging, I squeezed her fist in a silent urge to run far and fast away from me. The harder I gripped her, the better it felt until Letitia radiated from the corner of my eye, and I clenched my hand until Harlow's knuckles broke.

The girl—Harlow?—cried out.

"Kill her," Letitia snarled, inches from my face.

The track of my mind skipped and white noise filled my head as Letitia's fury seeped into my soul. That searing emotion became mine, and it was righteous. The mermaid was of no consequence. She was an obstacle to quenching my desire for vengeance.

Sweet anger flowed through my veins. I punched the girl in the solar plexus, and she shot backward like one of those hinged targets at the baseball toss booth at a carnival. She skidded across the clay, knees bent, and I climbed on her before she could sit upright. I hit her again. Her jaw popped. Again. Her head jerked to one side. Again. Blood cascaded from her nose over her lips.

"Idiot child."

I swatted my ear.

"Take my advice or you will take her life."

The nagging voice kept buzzing.

"Shadow and light canno' exist in ta same place at ta same time."

I clamped my hands over my ears.

Shadow and light. Shadow and light. Shadow and light.

The echo was maddening.

An image flickered in my mind's eye, a card drawn from the deck of my memories by the presence somehow rooted in my head. Two identical girls. Holding hands. Plush rabbits tucked under their arms. Matching dresses. Hair ribbons fluttered behind them.

One corner of the image caught fire. Flames engulfed one girl. *Lori*. My twin. My shadow.

"Perhaps you're no' a waste of oxygen after all."

The pressure in my skull vanished. The voice did too.

The moment of clarity was brutal. Harlow lay ruined and unconscious between my thighs.

"I didn't tell you to stop," the Fury seethed. "You aren't finished yet."

Yes, I was.

Lori was never more than a thought away. Not really. No matter how hard I tried to forget the gulf of loss her name inspired.

Becoming her such a short time ago only strengthened my bond to her form. I inhaled as Camille and exhaled as Lori.

Harlow's blood stained the hem of my nightgown. I scrambled off her and hid my face behind my hands. I let sobs crash through me, allowed my shoulders to shake with fear I didn't have to fake.

A dull thud sounded beside me.

"The hell, Tia?" a man's voice boomed. "What is she? A kid? You didn't say nothing about hurting no kid."

I peeked through my small fingers at him. The man had jumped into the basin to save me—or at least to determine if I deserved saving.

Choking out a cry, I ran to him and wrapped my arms around his legs. He patted my head while glaring down Letitia, who appeared torn too. She didn't want to hurt a kid, mothers were hardwired that way, and right about now she was thinking of her own rugrats. Even the shadow assigned to me faltered. That hesitation was all I needed.

The man wore jeans smeared with oil and smelling of diesel fuel. I reached up as if to take his hand, fingernail loosening, and pricked him with my spur. His blood sent faint tingles through my palm. *Witch.*

The man yelped and slung his hand in the air. "I think she bit me."

"No." Letitia pressed her fingers to her lips. "I saw her. She…"

A wealth of information streamed behind my eyes, years of this man's knowledge now written on the backs of my lids. A lifetime of magical theory swelled my brain, and the hairs lifted down my arms as I claimed his talents as my own.

Letitia was the first to read the situation. *"Get down."*

I flung a hand in her direction, a hex rising to my lips. She fell screaming and writhing. The man beside me I touched gently, and he sank to his knees in submission. The cheering and shouting I had gone deaf to vanished, leaving a void ringing in my ears.

"Who else?" I challenged.

The *umbras* hurled themselves at me. Mentally flipping through my options, I hit on a spell to banish darkness and yelled it as the shadows' murky forms descended on me. An orb of light ignited in my palm. Shocked by its sudden appearance, I hurled it at them before my skin blackened from the heat. Their maws opened in silent screams. Air displaced, and the night depressurized around me. The creatures were gone. When I glanced up, the nosebleed section stood empty. Footsteps and panicked shouts trailed after the cowards.

"Run," I slurred at them, wobbling on unsteady feet. So much knowledge crammed into a brain not hardwired for casting spellwork was fracturing my gray matter. My knees kept buckling. I was going down if I didn't get moving.

A fierce howl sent screams tearing through the night, and my heart flipped.

Graeson?

The stream of spellwork flickered and began fading from memory. Every step toward Harlow might as well have been a mile. Legs heavy, I forced my feet forward until I was in touching distance of her swollen cheek. Her secret was laid bare to me now. There was more to her story—there had to be—but for now she was a mortal with life-threatening injuries the witchy man knew how to cure. That *I* knew how to cure, for a few seconds more.

Cupping her battered face in my palms, I blew healing Words over her face. The exhale drained me. My lungs fought when I tried to refill them. The world tilted, and my head hit the ground. I was stretched out beside Harlow when her eyes opened, and I had a bird's-eye view while her torn flesh mended.

A heavy thud sprayed dirt over my face. The tiny grains of sand stung my eyes, so I shut them. A rough, wet tongue swept across my lashes. I pretended not to smell the coppery tang on the wolf's breath as he nudged me under the jaw with his cold nose. He wanted my eyes to open. I wanted them open too, but they were so heavy. The magic was gone. I was spent. I had nothing left.

A harsh grunt. A low groan. A voice strained by change managed, "Ellis?"

"Lori," I whispered, still trapped in her form.

"I've got you, sweetheart." Fingers trembling from the rapid shift, he clasped hands with me. "Rest. You're safe. I'm not going anywhere."

I'm pretty sure I told him *I'm not your sweetheart* before my consciousness slipped, because his rusty chuckles were the last thing I heard.

CHAPTER ELEVEN

Dreams didn't usually jar my teeth. The world dipped, and my head banged a hard surface. Light streamed through tinted windows and spilled over my face. The dull jab of a headache set up camp between my eyes. *Ouch.* I ground my palm into my forehead, gripped the back of a leather seat and leveraged myself upright.

"Where am I?" The question came out of me on a groan.

"An hour outside of Abbeville, Mississippi," a familiar voice replied on my right.

"Graeson?" I squinted at the blurry outline occupying the passenger seat.

"Call him Cord." The pale blue eyes of the driver flashed up to mine in the rearview mirror. Strawberry blonde hair sun-bleached with softer highlights. Flawless skin without a hint of makeup. An artful smattering of freckles that could have been hand-drawn for their symmetry. "Graeson makes him sound uptight."

The uptight warg in question grunted. "Ellis, this is Dell Preston."

"Short for Adele." She wiggled her eyebrows. "And *hi,* freaky shifter person."

Irritated prickles swept over my skin, and my fingers dug into the headrest. Too bad it wasn't Graeson's skull. "Freaky shifter person?"

"Dell," he growled.

"What?" Her forehead crinkled. "I'm a warg. You're a warg. It's not like shifter is a derogatory term."

"The freaky part is probably what she's taking exception to," he said dryly.

"Oh." Dell's lips pursed as she studied me instead of, oh, I don't know, the road. "Hi, totally *un*freaky shifter person."

"It's fine." The opinion of a random warg didn't matter one way or the other to me. "Where's Harlow?"

"She's on bedrest for the next twenty-four hours." He twisted around in his seat. "The magic you used healed her. You saved her life, Ellis."

"Who do you think escorted her to death's door?" I mashed my lips into a firm line. "I used to have better control." Vause was right about one thing, practice made perfect, and I was rusty. Relying on one of my talents to get by led to neglecting the others.

"That Fury would have killed her with or without your help." He placed a comforting hand on my knee and squeezed. "They don't back down. They'll self-destruct before stopping a hunt when they feel they've been slighted. You did the best you could. Harlow doesn't blame you, and you can't blame yourself."

He was wrong. Blaming myself was something I did very well.

"We got to you as fast as we could," the redhead offered.

"You were there too?" I searched my memories for a hint of a second wolf but found none.

"Cord was as pissed as a cat with firecrackers tied to its tail when I fished him out of the water. He'd swallowed half the lake, and partial drowning is tough for even a warg to recover from," she prattled on. A growl rose from the passenger seat, more felt than heard, but he didn't comment. "Anyway, I overheard the witch talking before y'all vanished. She called the shadow things her pets and said, 'Let's go home.' Graeson said home was Wink, Texas, so that's where we went. We booked a flight and—" she slapped the steering wheel with her palms, "—rented this big honking thing then went after you."

"Vanished?" I asked.

"I went to fetch Cord," she explained. "I didn't want the witch to get a head start, and I couldn't leave him behind. By the time we reached the spot where I last saw you, you were all gone. No scent. Nothing."

Just like in the woods. Either Letitia was an adept witch or she was friends with one to draw on magic so heavily to enact her revenge fantasy. The trip from Alabama to Texas was a long one, and I still didn't remember a blink of it. She must have drugged me or put a magical whammy on me.

"How did you two…? Are you…?" I stared at his proprietary hand on my knee, which seemed to have put Dell in a smug mood. "Why hasn't Graeson introduced us before now?"

"I didn't introduce you," he grumbled, "because I didn't know I'd been assigned a babysitter."

"Our alpha, Bessemer, had concerns about Cord's state of mind. He asked for volunteers to keep an eye on him, and my hand shot up in the air. I've been on his trail for days." Her grip tightened on the wheel. "Ever since…" A single tear slid down her cheek, glistening in the sunlight. She even cried prettily. "Anyway, I had a charm to hide my scent thanks to the brothers Garza, our pack witches, and I wouldn't have confronted him at all if you hadn't been taken."

Garza. I dedicated the name to memory. One of them must have been the brother-in-law he mentioned, the one with the kids using his body as a jungle gym.

As tempting as it was to ask what Dell's relationship was to Graeson, why she had been so eager to volunteer to shadow him, it was none of my business if Dell wanted to run around in the middle of nowhere, fishing waterlogged wargs out of lakes in the dead of night like some supermodel superhero.

"Mississippi, huh?" We passed a big green sign announcing we were fifty miles from Abbeville. Mississippi was a long drive from Texas. I recalled what Dell had said and noticed the takeout bags littering the floorboards. "You drove the whole way?"

"You needed rest." Graeson stroked the inside of my thigh with his thumb. "How much do you remember from yesterday?"

Thinking while he touched me required more mental acuity than I usually had while sleep crusted my eyes, but I didn't stop him, and I didn't let his caress unnerve me. Much.

I remembered the lake, the *umbras*, thinking Graeson had drowned. I recalled the basement, the igel, and almost ripping Harlow to pieces with my bare hands while trapped in a murderous rage. "All of it," I said quietly.

"Letitia used a teleportation spell to yank you back to Wink with her, in case you were wondering." He slid his seat belt down his shoulder so it wouldn't slice into his throat. "She wears a medallion with a piece of her home's hearthstone inside. A drop of blood, and bam. She's back home, safe and sound." A tight grin stretched his lips. "The marshals figured that part out when she vanished from her holding cell prior to her pat down."

Well that explained how she managed to snatch Harlow and then me. "How long was I out?"

"Twelve hours," Dell chirped. "Girl, let me tell you. You snore like a freight train. I live with wolves, and I've never heard anything like it. You should look into those sticky things you put on your nostrils to open your airways."

"Dell," Graeson rumbled.

"Um, I mean, on you it's cute." She flashed a smile. "You can totally get away with sounding like a runaway locomotive."

I cracked a grin at her rambling. For someone so polished on the outside, Dell had no trouble sticking her paw in her mouth once she started talking. "So what's in Abbeville?"

"The next victim," Dell answered.

Gorgeous and psychic too? Fate wasn't that cruel. Oh wait. Yes. It was. "Graeson?"

"I told you my brother-in-law is a witch." A frown touched his lips. "He's been casting divinations." He finally seemed to notice his hand was still on my knee, but he didn't move it. "We suspected Mississippi would be the next state targeted. Using the scale I found at the Brushy Creek scene as a focal point, he crafted a spell to pinpoint where the kelpie will strike next."

Not a bad plan, but it made no sense. "If it's that easy, then why didn't the conclave try it?"

Dell clicked her tongue. "We were wondering the same thing."

A chill settled in my bones. "You think they knew some of the locations prior to the attacks?"

"You said yourself that you expected the calls like clockwork. The conclave moves fast to cover fae tracks, but this would be record speed. The locations are remote, the search areas broad, and there aren't enough eyes on the ground to find the bodies on any type of schedule."

"It sounds like you don't trust the conclave," I said slowly, "so what am I doing here?"

Graeson withdrew his hand but left his fingers dangling over the console between the front seats while he watched my thoughts churn.

Lori. He still wanted to use her—*me*—to lure the kelpie.

I pressed my back against the seat. The absence of his hand left a chilly outline of his broad fingers through the fabric of my pants. "Does Vause know where I am?"

"Nope," Dell answered for him. "The less she knows the better."

I touched my pocket and found it empty. They had taken my phone. "Does that mean I can't check in?"

Graeson's mouth pinched. "We would prefer if you stayed out of touch for the next couple of days."

I pegged him with a glare. "You kidnapped me."

"We need your help."

"What about my family?" Pressure built behind my breastbone. "If the conclave can't locate me, they'll call my aunt." I gripped his wrist. "After what my family went through with Lori, I can't—I *won't*—let them think they've lost me too."

"Cut the girl a break," Dell murmured. "I mean, you did abduct her while she was unconscious."

"I brought her carry-on and laptop. I even grabbed that bag thing with the makeup in it." He made it sound like he'd done me some huge favor by not leaving my belongings to get stolen from my hotel room.

"Cord." Dell sounded pained.

"I'll let you call your aunt if you can keep a lid on your location," he agreed with reluctance.

"Great. I'm glad we got that settled. Any other orders you'd like me to follow? No, don't answer that. Of course there are." I resisted the urge to cross my legs in the confines of the backseat. "Does this mean I have to ask for permission to use the restroom too, 'cause I have to tell you, I'm about to pop."

"No." His gaze tagged Dell. "We have that covered."

"I inherited your babysitter." I huffed. "Great."

"Sorry." Dell hunched her shoulders. "For all of this."

"We have reinforcements meeting us in Abbeville," Graeson pressed. "You won't be operating alone. We won't let you get hurt."

"Reinforcements." It was too much to hope he would reach over Vause's head to ask the conclave for support. "I assume you mean your pack."

"Six of my best wolves." Pride warmed Graeson's voice. "You couldn't ask for better backup."

Eight wargs against one spellworking kelpie. "Your alpha doesn't mind that you're all off playing vigilante?"

"Bessemer obtained permission from the local alpha, as well as an offer of aid should we need more hands to take this thing down." Graeson twisted forward and gave the windshield his attention. "No one wants a creature who's preying on supernatural children loose in their backyard."

"Good. Fine. Whatever." I slumped against the door, propped my elbow on the armrest and peered through the glass. Nothing but trees, trees and more trees. "I was serious about the bathroom."

Dell applied the brakes and guided the SUV onto the side of the road. She leaned across Graeson, jerked open the glove box and fisted a handful of fast food napkins. She pressed them into my hand and disengaged the child safety locks I hadn't realized were on. "That ought to do it." She flicked her hand in a shooing gesture toward the tree line. "Go mark some territory, girlfriend."

CHAPTER TWELVE

The Chandler pack had commandeered an old bait-and-tackle shack that had, at some point, also served fast food. The scent of grease and fries clung to the air. After breathing in the calories for a few hours, I could have used a handful of antacids.

The wargs moved fast to organize their base camp. Our long drive from Wink had given them ample time to settle in and set Graeson's plans into motion. Plans I wasn't privy to. Not that I was bitter about being treated as cannon fodder or anything.

The witchy brother-in-law Graeson had mentioned, Miguel Garza, had set up shop at the now-defunct checkout counter. A younger man stood beside him, his face a dark shade of red from the blustering I had interrupted. Both had black hair, richly tanned skin and milk-chocolate eyes. Some of their more creative swearing called to mind the year I took Spanish in high school, but I pretended not to understand the insults being hurled like javelins lest I make myself a target for rolling my eyes at their dramatics.

Apparently the witches were debating the hour of the kelpie's attack. One, being a traditionalist, argued for midnight. The witching hour. The other, being more progressive, felt if a kelpie had committed eight previous murders in order to set a ritual circle, then its higher intelligence indicated it would hunt during times when children were more likely to be exploring unsupervised. He cast his vote for dusk. Five full hours earlier than the time Miguel suggested. And 'round and 'round they went.

"Are they always like this?" How did the pack stand the constant bickering with their sensitive ears?

"Pretty much," Dell, who stuck to me like a magnet on a fridge, confirmed. "You get used to it after a while. It becomes white noise. It's when they get quiet that you have to worry."

Tired of the sniping, I left the storefront and ventured back into the kitchen/bait-cleaning area. The narrow hall terminated in a grungy door. Scuffs and dents marred the brassy kick plate at its base. Long, thin lines of scratched paint bore testament to the number of times waitresses had dinged it with trays on their way through.

The tactical team—all six wargs—bent over maps they had spread over the countertops and weighted down with cans of pureed tomatoes. One tall woman sharpened a knife while a stout man fidgeted with his gun. Two steps into the kitchen, I attracted their attention. The annoyed vibe they cast in my direction sent me backing through the door. Must be a private meeting then.

One last bastion remained, and that was the staff break room outfitted with Wild West-style saloon doors. I let my feet guide me there as if that had been their intended destination all along.

I had showered off the blood and clay from the Rebec farm shortly after our arrival, then slept in a tiny closet masquerading as a studio apartment above the store. Coming downstairs had been a mistake. I should have known all roads would lead me right to Graeson.

"You're pacing tracks in the floor. Come in and sit down." His voice carried down the hall when I hesitated with a hand resting on one half of the set of swinging doors. "You're going to make yourself tired, and tired people make mistakes."

"Like trusting wargs?" I shoved inside and found him playing solitaire on a scuffed laminate tabletop, sitting in a chair with a warped leg. "Lesson learned. How about you let me go, and I forget about this whole unlawful-imprisonment thing you've got happening here?"

"You're the best chance we have at success." He thumbed the edge of his deck of cards. "Knowing what you know now, would you leave even if I gave you a set of keys?"

I didn't bother with an answer. It was a rhetorical question. There was no way I could bolt when he had intel pinpointing Charybdis's next move. Not when together we had the resources to stop him from taking another child's life.

I joined him at the table, and my leg bounced under it. "I need some answers. You said you want my help. Fine. How long is this operation of yours supposed to last? I can't stay off the grid for an entire month."

"You won't have to." His lips pursed while he debated his next move. "The Garzas are fighting out the timeline. We expect Charybdis to make his move within the next seventy-two hours."

"That breaks his pattern," I argued. "Isn't timing part of the ritual's magic?"

"The short answer is… We don't know. He takes his victims weeks prior to their discovery. The McKenna girl escaped. Losing her might have broken the pattern." He tapped a card on the table's edge. "Or, it's possible the dead girl Letitia claims to have seen with the kelpie was taken in time to be sacrificed on schedule."

I waved a finger through the air. "The Garzas can't wave a magic wand and tell us?"

"No." Reluctance flavored the word. "The purported victim's body won't be found for a few weeks, and if we're truly ahead of him, then by the time that girl is found the next will have already been taken."

Nodding that I understood, I still battled the feeling we had abandoned the poor girl, though a corpse was all we could have reclaimed had we stayed and searched for her.

"We're here because Miguel's magic said this is where the kelpie is or will be soon." He tilted his head. "The fact is, there are too many variables. We don't know enough about Charybdis to pinpoint any one thing as breaking his pattern. The conclave has never been a step ahead of him before." He flexed the card in his hand until it almost bent in two. "Coming to Mississippi so soon after a kill may be part of his process. He may be here scouting the area while he searches for potential complications prior to moving his operation here."

We were talking about a glorified horse thinking in terms that would be alien to an animal. This wasn't a run-of-the-mill kelpie, we knew that, but this wasn't the bipedal fae Thierry saw exit the portal either. Did that mean the portal fae was controlling the kelpie? To what end? What did he gain through having another creature commit murders on his behalf? Where did the circle fit into things? Why was Tennessee the target? We didn't have enough information to do more than guess, and guessing made for sloppy detective work.

We needed more from the Garza brothers. This was a good start, but it wasn't enough. We needed a means of tracking the person holding the kelpie's reins. The only way I could think of to do that was offering up the kelpie itself. Charybdis's magical signature permeated his victims' bodies long after death, but the trace was so faint I wasn't sure the witches could use the bodies we had recovered so far. Not to mention I couldn't very well sneak them into a secured conclave facility or smuggle one out for them to cast over. Our best bet was capturing the kelpie or, gods forbid, finding the remains of the Alabama girl before the conclave did, when they would be freshest.

Rolling my head on my neck, I rubbed my sore nape. "How long until the Garzas give us an update?"

"If they can't make up their minds soon, I plan on cracking their heads together." He thumped a card against the table. "We won't know the kelpie's whereabouts, but at least we'll be able to hear ourselves think."

I accepted that with a nod. "When do I get my phone call?"

"I'll drive you into town tonight. We'll pick up a burner cell and let you make your call." His expression didn't change. "Soon enough for you?"

"Yes," I said thoughtfully. Time to do some serious soul-searching. Did I want to go this alone? Did I trust Graeson and his pack to keep me safe? Or did I want to sneak a call in to Vause and bring in conclave reinforcements? "Am I allowed to go for a walk?"

"As long as Dell goes with you, sure." He didn't look away from his game. "Stick close to base."

The urge to slap him upside the head came and went on a sigh. I'd had my fill of alphahole for the night. Or was that betahole? Was there even a difference? I left Graeson to his cards and hit the rattletrap porch. Dell, who had been hovering in the hall, fell in step behind me.

Violet clouds bruised the pink sky. Water glittered on my left. I turned right.

"So…" Dell scooped up a rock and hurled it bouncing down the road ahead of us. "What are you exactly?"

"Graeson didn't tell you?"

"Don't call him Graeson, seriously. That last-name thing you cops do is weird." She wrinkled her nose. "I did ask him what species of fae you are. I figured if I was helping him kidnap you, I ought to at least know how much trouble we stood to get into with the conclave over you. Cord told me to mind my own damn business."

"You called me a freaky shifter." Those had been among the first words out of her mouth to me. "I assumed that meant you watched the show out at the Rebecs' place."

"Well, see, we decided to go in fangs out. We're scarier on four legs than two," she said conversationally. "It turns out the Rebecs raised chickens. Some guy saw me coming and flung open the pen." She licked her lips. "I might have chased the hens down and eaten them instead of providing backup." She offered me a shrug. "Cord said he had it covered, and how often do you find all-you-can-eat chicken buffets?"

"Raw chicken?" Now it was my turn to wrinkle my nose. "Never, I hope."

Her brows waggled at me. "Don't knock it 'til you try it."

A chorus line of salmonella danced through my head. "I'll pen that onto my to-do list."

She sank her elbow into my side and dug it in to the bone. "Come on. Spill. You've got to have some kind of super-cool talent for Cord to be so nutso about you." She bent and snagged another rock. "You should have seen him at the Rebec place. He was all but salivating over you. I figured you must be dead." She winced. "Not that we go around killing and eating people—it's bad press—but accidents happen. Meat is meat. I just mean he doesn't much care for non-wargs, but he went ballistic when that Fury came to. I thought he was going to rip her—" As though sensing my unease—maybe she smelled it?—Dell dropped that line of thought. "So…anyway…you were about to tell me all about you."

"I'm a Gemini."

"Like the constellation, right?" She drew squiggles in the air to represent the stars. "What makes a Gemini a Gemini?"

I stopped walking and stuck out my hand. "Want to find out?"

"I asked, didn't I?" She clasped palms with me without hesitation. "Now what?"

The spur in my fingertip slid from its sheath, the nail falling to the ground, and I pricked the back of her hand, between the knuckles. The wild tang of her blood flooded my veins, and a buzzing noise poured into my head. I barely heard her exclamation as a thick, golden pelt sprouted from my black-clawed fingertips up to my elbow, the spur receding as a claw took the place of that missing fingernail.

"*Whoa.*" Dell poked her button nose under my jaw. "You even smell like a warg. Kind of like me. Like a sister or cousin or something. Is that it? Can you do more? Can you shift into a wolf? Can you shift into *my* wolf?" The implications caught up to her. "Wait—does this mean you can copy anything?"

I held up a hand to halt the avalanche of questions. "Yes, I can do more. No, I can't fully shift. And yes, I can copy any supernatural talent." I rubbed my ear with the unclawed hand. "What is that sound?"

Dell took my paw in her hand, flipping it over and stroking the tawny fur, which soothed me the way a good foot massage might. "You'll have to be more specific."

"Voices." I focused on the noise. "But not voices. There are so words. There's just…presence."

When I closed my eyes to focus, a ribbon of shimmering pavement stretched in my mind's eye from here past the horizon. Warmth spread through my chest, filling jagged cracks left from Lori's loss. The void still yawned in her absence, but the flaming light penetrated the absolute darkness that had shrouded me for so long. For a second or two I felt…at peace.

The wonder in Dell's eyes distracted her as the pelt fell out in clumps. "It's the pack bond." She touched my cheek. "I didn't notice before—I was distracted—but I can feel you." A grin blossomed. "That's *amazing*."

As though her touch amplified the connection, I rested my face in her hand, absorbing the sensation of belonging. The burn in my fingertips as my fingernails regrew made me grimace. The comfort I had so briefly tasted scattered, and I was alone in my head again. A spike of grief swelled in my chest as I mentally grasped at what I could no longer perceive. The psychic feedback slammed into the walls of my skull and throbbed.

Amazing was one word for it. To think wargs experienced that every moment of their lives filled my mouth with a bitter taste. Another time I might have called it jealousy.

I withdrew from Dell and turned my back on her while I pulled myself together. She kept pace beside me, seeming to understand I needed a moment alone. The rest of our walk passed in silence except for the chittering songs of cicada, though I caught her staring at me out of the corner of her eye more than once. When the buzz of mosquitoes became too loud to ignore and my face and neck grew lumpy and itchy, I accepted defeat and returned to the bait shack.

Graeson met us on the steps, a shoulder braced against one of the weathered two-by-fours supporting the bowed roof. If the red dots covering his arms were any indication, he had been waiting on our return for a while. "Enjoy your walk?"

My gaze slid past him to my home away from home for the next however long my kidnapping lasted. "Yes." I smiled thinly. "The dirt road is one of the more scenic ones I've walked, and I've never seen bird-sized mosquitos before."

A cool breeze off the water twirled loose hairs into my eyes. Graeson shot down the steps before I could pat them back into place. His hands cinched my upper arms, and he lifted my feet almost off the ground. His nose traced the length of my jaw, his breaths warm on my neck, his lips soft against my skin. Chills raced along the same path. I didn't move. I barely breathed.

Having a carnivore pay that kind of close attention to me was enough to turn my knees to water. Good thing he was holding me upright.

"What are you doing?" That breathy voice was *not* mine.

"You smell female." His words rumbled at my ear.

"I *am* female." I planted my hands on his abs, which was as high as I could reach with my arms locked at my sides, and pushed him back. Or tried to. I had no leverage, and he didn't budge an inch. "Thanks for noticing."

"A *warg* female." He examined every inch of my exposed skin as though he expected to glimpse the fur I had shed earlier. "It was you." His grip eased. "I came outside because I sensed… But that's not possible."

"She partially shifted." Dell presented her hand for his inspection, though the wound I had inflicted on her had long since healed. "It was very cool. Too bad we don't have anything more interesting for her to shift into. We see wargs all the time. We ought to—"

Graeson tore his gaze from me. "Ellis is not a toy for you to play with."

Dell cringed at his tone, and her chin bumped her chest.

"Don't snap at her." I kicked his shin. "Dell didn't do anything wrong."

Those fierce golden eyes settled on me, and I fought the impulse to run when he set me back on my feet. Graeson still gripped my arms, and his thumbs stroked my skin absently. "There are dynamics within a pack you don't understand."

Dynamics sounded like code for belittling females. In which case, I understood plenty.

"I'm ready for that trip into town." I glared at his hands and gave a wiggle. "That means you have to let go of me."

He released me with a shake of his head, and I left him staring at his hands as though blaming them for the red marks on my arms. "We have to wait a few more hours. Knox took the SUV on a supply run."

"What about the vans?" There were two of them parked behind the house. I saw them when we first arrived, but I hadn't spotted them again since.

"The vans are Chandler pack property, and the tags are registered with the conclave and several other fae organizations that get nervous around native supernats." The gravel in his words told me exactly what he thought about that. "I don't want our presence advertised around town."

"Yes," I agreed, "it would be a shame if the conclave mounted a rescue mission, wouldn't it?"

"You're hardly a prisoner," he said with a sour twist of his lips, as if he didn't quite believe what he was saying. That made two of us.

"You captured me and brought me along for the ride." I shifted my stance. "The only thing holding me here is the possibility we might end this before another child is taken."

Graeson looked like he wanted to argue, but he wisely kept his mouth shut.

"I'm heading inside to see if I can find something to stop the itching." I scratched my arms lightly with my nails. "Come get me when you're ready to leave."

"Ellis."

I faced him, eyebrow arched, and waited.

"I wish that you and I…" He clamped his mouth shut, spun on his heel and strode into the cover of darkness without another word.

Despite my best efforts, I hung on his words. What sort of wishes did he harbor for us? Regret, I was learning, wasn't a strong enough emotion to deter him from accomplishing his goals. He would use me, and he might regret it later. No. He *would* regret it, but he had me where he wanted me, and he wasn't about to let a small thing like a wish he couldn't verbalize stand in his way.

Dell followed me inside but a male caught her eye, and she crossed to him with halting steps. I waited to see what it was about, but she waved me on with a bright smile that didn't warm her eyes, and I went because Graeson was right. There were dynamics here I didn't understand, and the last thing I wanted was to get Dell hurt by sticking my nose where it didn't belong.

Once in my room, I flopped onto the cot, thoughts circling back to Dell and my partial shift. I relived that sparkling moment of connectivity. The pack bond had glittered in my mind like a serpentine trail winding toward… I wasn't sure. Contentment? Serenity? Happiness? What might have happened to me if I'd followed the path? Would I have been embraced by it? Absorbed into the collective? What shimmering promise awaited all who found their feet planted on that diamond-dust road?

All the *what might have beens* were as bittersweet as the memory of Graeson's feverish caress. He shouldn't have handled me that way. Not when he barely knew me. Not when I wasn't pack. He was confused by that brief mental trespass across the pack collective. That was all.

I lifted my hand and turned it back and forth. The thought of shifting into a wolf who could outrun my problems was all too tempting. How lucky Graeson was to have a beast to share his burden.

The shack's previous owner had skimped on the insulation, which meant I had no problem picking out the rhythmic crunching of gravel invading my thoughts. It sounded like more than two pairs of boots. A set of wargs? Sentries maybe? I shoved to my feet and yanked the soiled tablecloth-turned-curtain away from the cramped window.

A white horse ambled across the parking lot. Preternatural energy flowed around it, buffeting its mane and tail in an unearthly breeze. It stamped its front leg and tossed its head, beckoning me with its liquid eyes, black and gleaming. Taunting me. My fingers pressed into the cool glass. I hadn't realized my arm lifted until my index finger traced the curve of its spine through dust caking the glass. That spike of cold shocked me aware, and I jerked my hand back.

A final snort and the apparition made a wide turn. Its movements were awkward, like its hooves were sucked into wet sand with every step. Its tail flicked and ears swiveled as its entire body shuddered. Mosquitoes. Horseflies. Something made its hide twitch.

A flash of blue. Short cotton nightgown. Tumble of wild chestnut hair. A small hand stuck to the kelpie's flank.

It looked like we wouldn't need Lori after all.

"Graeson." I slapped the glass with my open palm. *"Graeson."*

I hit the stairs at a run and almost tumbled the last four steps. I barreled past Dell, who straddled the male warg's lap while he growled into her ear, and called louder for Graeson. Drawn by the commotion, the other wargs piled into the narrow hall. I waded through their bodies, avoiding their grasping hands and their questions.

The break room doors slapped the walls as Graeson shoved through them. Gold sparked in his gaze, and his lip quivered as he clamped his hands on my shoulders. "What happened? Did someone...?"

"No." I sank my nails into his biceps. "It's here," I said loud enough for all to hear. "The kelpie is in the parking lot."

"Where are Revelin and Torin?" he snapped.

"Running the perimeter last I saw," Dell said, straightening her clothes and her spine. "I'll find them."

"You do that. Bring their asses to me. Secure the area," he barked at the others. "Don't let it escape."

Fear curled in my gut. "It's taken a new girl."

Bones popped in his hands where they touched me. "Was she alive?"

"Yes." Though she wouldn't be for long unless we caught up to them. "She was walking under her own power." I pushed against him, propelling us both out the door. "Be careful if you catch up to them. Like the McKenna girl, her hand is stuck to its hide."

"Stay put." He bolted onto the porch. "Dell will keep an eye on you."

A silent figure slipped to my side. She still wouldn't look him in the eye.

Graeson melted into the night, and wolves in various stages of change followed him. Soon Dell and I were the only ones left, and I was itching to join the others. Was this the end? Would this girl's death close the circle if we failed to save her? What happened then? I couldn't stand here twiddling my thumbs and wait for Graeson to bring me back an answer.

My stock had plummeted with the kelpie's arrival. Lori was no longer required. I should have felt relieved to be off the hook, but guilt sat heavy in my gut that I might have spared this girl had we moved faster. "How does he expect me to play bait if he won't let me out of his sight?"

I didn't expect an answer—I was venting—so I was surprised when she offered one.

"He's relieved," she said, soft enough to evade sensitive warg ears. "He didn't want to send you out there. This means he won't have to."

Dell was wrong. Her trust in Graeson blinded her to the brutal core of him. I had no such illusions.

"Just so you know," I informed her as I took the steps, "I'm not waiting here."

Graeson ought to know better. You'd think a dominate warg would understand how being told to *sit* and *stay* would chafe.

"Cord said—"

"This is my job. This is what I do." The wood steps groaned under my weight. "Are you coming or staying?"

"But *Cord*—"

“I’m not a warg. He’s just a man in need of a mood stabilizer and a bottle of Nair as far as I’m concerned.”

“I…” She bit her lip. “I just— I don’t think...”

“I can’t wait.” My voice came out raw. “That girl needs me. She needs all the help she can get.”

Alone, I marched into the night. I had run once. I wouldn’t run again. I wouldn’t be content to sit and wait while others did the heavy lifting. I was here. The kelpie had taunted *me*. I was not going to cower and cost that girl another set of eyes in the search. I would not be standing on this porch, too far away to do any good, when she snapped from her fugue and cried for help.

“I’ll get in more trouble if I let you wander alone than for letting you stray in the first place.” Dell caught up to me without breaking a sweat. “I’ve got your back.” She puffed up her already impressive chest. “While you’re with us, you’re pack.” She synced her strides with mine. “Pack means no one stands alone.”

Walking next to her, knowing she meant what she said, I had never felt lonelier.

CHAPTER THIRTEEN

Hours later the mud caking my shoes made each squelching step burn in my thighs and calves. The aroma of dead fish washed ashore to rot polluted the muggy air. I trudged on, but the night stretched for eternity out here, and I lost all sense of direction. I felt the absence of my cell phone keenly. The GPS app would have helped. So would the ability to call for backup once the kelpie made its presence known.

Calling Vause was reflex. I would have done it without thought. Cut off from that access, I had time to think about the fact the witches had been right. One scale had given them Charybdis's location. How many scales must the conclave have in evidence by now? How much other organic detritus that could power a divination or locator spell? So why hadn't they found him? Stopped him? Why was he allowed to continue on unchecked? Why bother with the ruse of a cleanup crew at all if they had no intentions of capturing him?

The circle must be the key. If Charybdis was being allowed to hunt, then it meant one thing. The conclave wanted that circle set, but why? As a magistrate, Vause was in this plot up to her neck, she had to be. That meant I couldn't trust her with the kelpie's whereabouts. Not until I understood the stakes of the game we all played. For now Graeson and I would see this through, together, and we would decide how to handle the beast once we captured it.

Fae were an invasive species as far as most wargs were concerned. Even without the urge to avenge his sister riding him, Graeson didn't strike me as the kind of man who would risk turning the kelpie over to the conclave for punishment. He was mistrustful of them and would take matters into his own claws if I didn't stop him first. The problem being I was having trust issues myself.

A honey-colored wolf ranged in wide circles, stopping now and then to move in for a scratch between the ears before darting off in pursuit of rodents. I had left exploration of the lake to the pack and headed inland on the off chance the kelpie had decided to flee the area after its brazen display. What had been the point of revealing itself? What was it trying to tell us? Show us? Or was I being paranoid, and it simply happened to cross our path?

Yeah. Right.

I lumbered over soggy ground and prayed the snakes kept to themselves. There were water moccasins in the area. The wargs had killed one near the porch. It was a petty concern in the grand scheme of things, but fearing the burn of venom from their bite helped distract from the sound of lapping waves and the fact mud slurped at my boots because I was in spitting distance of a massive body of water.

The ocean roared. Sand caked my feet. Lori screamed.

I crammed the past down before it choked me, and carried on.

As the pink fingers of dawn striated the sky, I came across a well-worn trail and thanked my lucky stars. It was packed higher than the surrounding area and sloped to drain. I stepped onto the path and followed it out of sight of the water until I reached a campground. Already I breathed easier. I gestured for Dell to hang back while I investigated.

Hunting wasn't my thing. Fae didn't need guns or permits. Their teeth and claws worked just fine. But I was pretty sure humans were allowed to hunt in certain tracts of national forests, which Charybdis frequented, and I had no clue if I should expect armed campers or not based on the season. Wolves weren't on the menu for humans, I didn't think, but I wasn't about to take a chance on Dell getting hurt in case they mistook her "tame" behavior as sickness.

Picnic benches cozied up to simple black grills cemented into the ground on thick metal posts. A gleaming RV had claimed one slot in the modest lot marked with six parking spaces. A battered truck with a ratty camper shell occupied another. At the far end a boxy red subcompact car took up a space beside a simple dome tent pitched in the spot next to it.

A teenager with sleep-matted hair bulldozed me. "Have you seen a young girl?" Her fingers dug into my forearms. Delicate magic tickled my skin. Her classification popped into my head. *Sylph.* "This high? Brown hair? No? Did you see anyone in the water?"

Dread sent my stomach crashing into my toes, and I proceeded carefully. "Did you lose someone?"

"*No.* I didn't lose her." She blinked rapidly. "She knows we're leaving this morning. She probably went to the lake to look for her stupid fish." A tear rolled down her cheek. "Her mask is here. She never goes anywhere without it."

I kept my voice level. "Her fish?"

"My sister caught a brim yesterday. It was her first catch. When she saw the hook in its mouth…" The girl heaved a long-suffering sigh. "She wanted to release it, but I'm not great with getting them off the hook. Its cheek tore. She begged me to let her keep it. She wanted to take it to a vet. The fish was hurt, and I didn't want to deal with tears if it died, so I tossed it back before she could stop me. She's been trying to find it again to check on it. I had to pull her out of the water last night."

"I need you to take a deep breath, okay? I'm here to help, but I have to ask you a few questions. Did you hear anything strange last night?" The pitiful cries of an animal in distress… "Did you see anything unusual?"

"N-no." She wiped her cheeks dry, and her red-rimmed eyes focused on me for the first time. I saw the moment she processed I wasn't just another camper. I was too calm, and I asked too many questions. Ones she knew instinctively involved her missing sister. "Who are you?"

"Camille Ellis. I work for the Earthen Conclave."

"I'm Daphne Tanner. My sister is Veronica." Her voice went soft. "Roni."

Roni Tanner. Another name etched into my memory. I hoped like Elizabeth McKenna, I would remember her as a girl who survived, and not one who was fallen.

"Are you familiar with the area?" I guided the young woman toward a composite bench, the type made from recycled plastic, and we sat across from one another. "What brought you out here?"

"I'm attending college out of state. I came home for the weekend, and Roni begged to go camping. Just us girls. Our folks come up here all the time, but they have an RV. It's not really camping when you can watch TV and walk around in your bathrobe, you know?" Her gaze lit on their tent. "I can't drive the RV anyway. It's huge, and the roads out here…" Her bottom lip trembled. "Roni was guilt-tripping me about never spending time with her, so I borrowed a tent from a friend." She glanced over at me. "One night. That was it. How did this happen?"

I took her hand and squeezed her fingers. "Walk me through what happened last night."

"We ate around six. Roni was bored, and she wanted to search for that damn fish one more time before bed, but I was tired. I told her no. She wouldn't listen when I said it had swam off to be with its family." She made a wriggling motion with her hand. "I was scared it might be floating belly-up on top of the water if she went looking. I've been studying for finals, so I was wiped. I didn't want more drama. We went to bed around eight. I should have heard her when she left the tent. She had to step over my head to get out, but I don't know. She must have sneaked past me."

Working under the assumption the kelpie's actions were being orchestrated by a magic user, it made sense they might also be casting sleep enchantments on the victims' families. All the better to lure the young and curious without getting caught.

"Is more help coming?" Daphne scanned the road behind me with a hopeful expression.

"I dropped my cell," I lied. "I'll have to wait for my backup to find me." Her crestfallen acceptance forced me to act the part. Even if it got me in hot water with Graeson. "Unless… Do you have a phone I can borrow?"

"Sure." She whipped it from her back pocket and pressed it into my hand. "I disabled the password so Roni could play games. Just swipe the lock screen and then dial."

Possibilities and repercussions cascaded through my head as my fingers closed over the slim phone. This gave me an out if I wanted one. It meant I could call a cab and go home, leave the conclave to tidy up their own messes. Dialing in also meant placing a grief-stricken warg who had taken his vendetta too far into custody until the magistrates decided on a punishment for abducting one of their own. Graeson wasn't in his right mind, kidnapping me proved that, but he was thinking clearer than Vause seemed to be. As tempting as it was to steal that promised call to Aunt Dot or leave the wargs to their scheming, I had to see this through. I was done running when others needed my help.

"Do you mind if I walk up the road a bit?" I propped my lips into a smile. "I'd prefer some privacy to make the call."

"Oh. Sure." Her brows pulled into a deep *V* in the center of her forehead. "I'll go wait in the car."

"Great." I swiped my thumb and dialed random numbers. "I'll handle this as quickly as possible so we can get more eyes out for your sister."

Nodding, Daphne turned and started walking back to her vehicle. I took the road and made a beeline for the trees where I last saw the golden wolf. I needed Graeson, and his wasn't a number I could dial. It wasn't like wolves carried phones in their fur suits. We'd have to do this the old-fashioned way, through a howl-o-gram.

"Dell." I rustled a shrub with my foot. "*Dell.*" I shook a tree limb. "I need to get in touch with Graeson. Can you do that mind thing and send him a message?" Pitiful whimpers lured me deeper into the undergrowth. "Dell?"

"Right…" a drawn-out grunt, "…here."

A pale figure curled into the fetal position rocked on the damp carpet of the forest floor. I shoved through the dense undergrowth and knelt at her side. "Are you all right?"

Her stiff limbs extended one by one, joints popping into alignment, until she managed to roll onto her back. Sweat slicked her skin, and her bare breasts jiggled from her shortness of breath. "I'm good." She sprawled nude in the dirt without a hint of modesty and picked a skeletal leaf from her hair. "I can ring up Cord from here."

"You're going to howl like this?" The shock of finding her naked popped the words out of my mouth before my brain caught up to them. Unlike with Graeson, whose nakedness inspired bone-deep female appreciation, Dell's nudity called my protective instincts to the fore. I would have offered her my jacket to cover herself if I'd worn one today.

"Um, no. That's not how we operate." She snorted. "Besides, we need to keep a low profile until the others arrive. Howling in wolf form would announce our position. Howling in human form, well, that's not something that happens without four or five cases of beer involved."

The pack bond. A *ping* of thought bounced off the inside of my skull before I realized I had reached out on reflex to grasp that golden highway before slamming into a roadblock. *Damn it.* One taste of their connection should not have left me starving for more.

Dell lifted her arm, clearly reading my mind without help from the bond, a smile dancing on her lips. "Or…you can tell him yourself."

I stared at her hand and wet my lips. What if it didn't work this time? What if the first spark had been a fluke? Such decadent inclusion could become addictive to a loner like me. It was no replacement for the twin bond, or for the parents who had abandoned me. Even in the presence of many, I ached with their absence. I always would, and no amount of warg blood could change that. All it could do was show me exactly what I was missing.

"No." I wiped my damp palms on my pants. "You can handle this."

I didn't think I could endure the loss of that blissful state of communion if I achieved it again.

"Oh." She pushed herself upright. "Okay." She blinked and stared at me, waiting. "I got him. What do you want to pass along?"

"Tell him we're at a campground near the lake."

"Give him a minute." She flushed. "He's exhausting his vocabulary of curse words." The idea of Graeson losing his cool over my audacity to ignore his orders coaxed a grin out of me. Dell cleared her throat and lowered her voice to a suitably masculine octave, the better to mock him with. "I'm not above cuffing you to the bed, Ellis. Don't defy my orders again."

"Wouldn't dream of it." I rolled my eyes and ignored the bed comment.

Dell smothered a girlish laugh then switched back to Graeson. "Can you be more specific?"

"Hold that thought." I hiked back to the path and glanced around for signs. *Bingo*. Someone had used a scroll saw to write Upper Branch Campground into a weathered rectangle of wood nailed to a tree trunk. I returned to Dell and relayed the information. "That's as specific as I can get without a phone or a compass."

Dell's gaze latched on to my hand where I clutched the cell, but I cut her a murderous glare and hoped she could keep Graeson from plucking the mental picture from her head. I wasn't sure how deep he was dug in there, but I didn't want to be chewed out later.

"We'll be there in five minutes," Dell-as-Graeson said.

"I'm going to stay with Daphne until the pack arrives," I told them, eager to wipe my prints off the phone and return it to its rightful owner. "I don't want the sight of wolves to spook her." Or to give her the wrong idea about her sister's fate.

Leaving Dell to wait for Graeson and the other wargs, I sought out Daphne. I found her sitting in the driver's front seat of her car with the door propped open. Red-and-white tennis shoes were planted firmly on the ground. She had braced her elbows on the armrest built into her door. Her shoulders were jumping with the force of her muffled sobs.

Each of her pitiful cries drove the knife deeper into my chest. I had been here before, been the sister who survived, the one who had to face down expectant parents and explain what happened to their other daughter, their baby. I hoped Daphne's mother and father were more understanding than mine had been, and if we failed to save Roni, I prayed they were more forgiving.

Tragedy was losing one child by chance. Travesty was losing a second by choice.

CHAPTER FOURTEEN

Lunch at the bait shack consisted of hamburgers, wings, footlong hotdogs, fried chicken and, oddly enough, bologna. A buffet of the finest fried foods available in Abbeville. The pack wolfed down the meat and gnawed the marrow from the bones, in human form, but the extra crispy thigh I had picked apart with my fingers never made it past my lips.

Two pack members had escorted Daphne home after Graeson assessed the situation. A male had packed her things and driven her car to the address listed on her driver's license, and the female whose name I hadn't caught gave Daphne a ride in the van because she had no longer been speaking or doing much of anything but staring into the distance while tears rolled silently down her cheeks by that point.

The female borrowed my badge and a business card, and then memorized my cell phone number so if the Tanners had questions they would dial her—*me*—instead of hunting down a representative from the local marshal's office. The quieter we kept this, the better. Even with the Tanners assured we were doing our best, we had a tiny window to produce results before Mrs. Tanner raised a ruckus over her missing daughter. A sobering thought considering how it was my name and badge number she would recite if questioned about the phony marshal visit.

Across the room, Graeson sat in a far corner staring out a broken window into the marsh. A paper plate piled high with food rested on his knees, but he hadn't eaten a bite. The others pretended not to notice, but I stared, hoping the weight of my gaze would turn his head and we could talk about where to go from here. But his attention belonged to the swaying grasses, not to me.

Slurping noises brought my attention back to Dell, whose face was smeared with hot sauce. A wing bone stuck to her bottom lip, and she chewed one end the way a farmer might grind a wheat stem between his teeth.

The makeshift table wobbled when I nudged my plate across it. "I need to clear my head."

The bone fell onto her lap. "But the food will be gone when we get back."

"That's okay." Careful not to jar the others at the table, I stood and inched past them. "I'm not hungry."

"Well, I am." She grabbed a handful of napkins and wiped her face. Most of the sauce had dried and stuck to her chin. "Come on, Camille. Ten minutes. Just long enough for me to go for fourths. I'll never make it to fifths with this crowd."

The itch beneath my skin intensified the longer I stood there with the wargs staring at me. The pack bond at work no doubt. Gossiping about the kidnapee where she couldn't hear them. How polite. The female warg tucked her plate to her chest and released a warning growl. Before the nearest man could stop me, I snagged an entire untouched bucket of chicken, thrust it into Dell's arms and started walking.

"Hey," he protested.

"Haden." One word from Graeson ended the quarrel before it began.

I withered Haden with a glance and then hit the porch as though the pack were nipping at my heels. Or worse, its beta. The muggy air stank of old house and wet dog. The wolves had been in the water again, scenting the sandbars for fresh signs the kelpie had passed through. When the kelpie's scent trail had vanished at the edge of the parking lot, the Garzas suspected magical intervention, but there was no handy Fury to blame this time.

The longer we chased Charybdis the more convinced I became he and the kelpie were two separate entities working toward a common goal. Catching two killers was a daunting prospect since I had only ever registered one magical signature at the crime scenes. We had blamed the erasure spell in Alabama on the Fury, but maybe we were wrong. Maybe it was Charybdis scrubbing his presence from the kelpie's kill sites so the conclave focused on the killer responsible for the wet work.

A whiff of jasmine and honeysuckle hit my nose. I descended the steps and set off in search of the origin. Why not? I had nothing better to do. No books. No TV. No Internet. No phones. Wargs didn't need them to communicate, but I was getting twitchy without my cellphone and its distracting apps.

Paper shredded, and I heard Dell inhale over the bucket. "I'm ready to go home. My meemaw's chicken is so much better than this."

"I know what you mean." Not the chicken part. Aunt Dot wasn't allowed in the kitchen unsupervised. The poor woman could burn water. The going-home part? That sounded good right about now. Graeson still owed me a phone call, but last night was riding us hard today, and I wasn't ready to do battle for that promised trip into town.

I was starting to regret not using Daphne's cell while I had the chance. Paranoia had warned me the conclave might trace her phone records to corroborate her story, and the last thing I wanted to explain was why I hadn't reported the incident or checked in with Vause. Letting Aunt Dot worry a while longer seemed the lesser of two evils.

"Where's home for you?" she asked around a hunk of breast meat.

"Tennessee is where I live now."

A thoughtful crunch. "You're not from there originally?"

A twinge rippled through my chest. "No."

"Do you live alone?"

"Yes and no. Home is an airstream trailer." I smiled thinking of its cozy quarters. "My aunt and cousins live in the same RV park as I do. Aunt Dot bought it, actually. It looked like I would be stationed there for a while, and she wanted a new project. She kind of collects real estate from all the places we visit."

"Huh." The bucket rattled when she jogged to catch up to me. "You mean your whole family goes where your job sends you?"

"Gemini are nomadic by nature." We also tended to band together in family groups. "With Aunt Dot getting older, it's easier to have time to plan our next move and coordinate."

"Are you seeing anyone?" Dell munched thoughtfully. "All that travel has to be rough on relationships."

"I don't date, so it's not a problem," I assured her. Dell's chicken must have gone down the wrong pipe, because she started choking. I whacked her on the back, and she caught her breath after a minute. "Are you all right?"

"Yes," she wheezed. "I just— That sounds lonely."

Lonely I was used to. Having company outside of blood relatives…now that was weird. First Harlow and now Dell and the ever-present Graeson. "Are you seeing anyone?"

"No." With a grunt of effort, she hurled her chicken bone into a tree trunk. "My last boyfriend found his lifemate at the grocery store. I sent him out for frozen custard, and he came home with a leggy brunette named Petra." She selected a wing. "The worst part? He forgot the custard." She bit down hard. "Bastard."

"Don't you want the mated thing?" I assumed all wargs would be excited for the hunt. "That whole fated soul-mate connection?"

"Eh." Another bite. "The idea of a random stranger walking up to me one day and saying, 'Hey, baby, you smell like forever. Let's do it,' isn't all that appealing honestly."

A snort escaped me. "Yeah, I guess not."

"Not everyone is a traditionalist." She rattled the bucket and plunged a hand inside. "Some wargs are already in relationships or married when their destined mate shows up on the doorstep. Some of them say no. At least at first."

I hummed in my throat. "That sounds like a heartache waiting to happen."

"Sometimes," she conceded. "I'm just saying, if you meet a male and like what you see, that you shouldn't write him off because of what *might* happen."

I tripped over my own feet. "Tell me you aren't playing matchmaker."

"All I'm saying is Cord's in my head, and he's got a one-track mind where you're concerned, if you catch my drift."

Prickles stung my cheeks. "That's not possible." I gestured around us. "All of this is for Marie. He must be thinking of her. After Lori…" I rubbed the ache under my breastbone. "I was crazed for months. It was all I thought about."

The quirk of her brow made me think Graeson hadn't told her about Lori, which earned him bonus points in my book. It was one thing to be a kidnapper. It was another to be a blabbermouth.

"Is the connection always so wide open?" That must make pack life awkward. "Can you all read each other's minds?"

"Uh, well. It's like this." Her gaze darted left to right. "There's something you should know about that."

"Dell." The low voice resonated in my bones. "I'll take it from here."

The bucket of chicken groaned where she squeezed it against her chest. "I'll wait for you on the porch."

What I hoped passed for a comforting smile bent my lips. She ducked her head and spun on her heel. She couldn't get out of there fast enough. I didn't blame her. Alone with Graeson was pretty far down my list of favorite places to be too.

"Do you always walk this much?" Accusation throbbed in his tone. "Or is this a recent development?"

Now that Dell had piqued my interest, I studied him for hints of what she had been about to say. The fatigue etching his face had lessened. The grief that had clung to him when we met, he kept behind a wall that I struggled to see over. His eyes were still dull, but I had witnessed flashes of their brilliance. I wasn't sure what it meant that he concealed his pain so well. What else might he be hiding?

"I move around a lot. I have a high-stress job." I pegged him with a glare. "I've also been kidnapped by a renegade cell of rogue wargs. That's enough to make a girl antsy."

"We're taking good care of you." Graeson stepped forward, and sunlight cast shadows under his hollowed cheeks. "We're providing for you."

Call me crazy, but the subtext rang loud and clear. That *he* was the one doing the providing. Must be some alpha he-man impulse.

I stood my ground. "Haven't you ever heard the saying that a gilded cage is still a cage?"

"You're not rattling your bars too loudly. We both know you could leave at any time. Say the word, and I'll drive you to the airport myself." His jaw flexed, as if he had to force out the offer. "You could have used that girl's phone at Upper Branch. Yeah, I saw it in your hand through Dell's thoughts." Another step closer when my cheeks flamed. I *knew* that would bite me on the butt. "Why didn't you?"

"A girl is missing." I tilted up my chin. "I owe her the best chance at being found, and right now that's you and me."

"I like the sound of *us*," he growled softly.

Graeson towered over me, his warm breaths hitting my cheeks. They were rapid and deep, drawing in my scent. His golden eyes burned until all I wanted to do was blink, but I knew he would view it as submission, and I wasn't bending an inch where he was concerned. He cupped the side of my neck. One of his large hands, warm and calloused, pulled me forward. My gaze held steady, and the challenge in his made my stomach quiver. My hands hovered over his chest, almost touching but not ready to concede to tactile curiosity. When his head lowered, he kept his lips a whisper above mine, daring me to close the gap and take what he offered.

"Cord."

I jerked out of his grasp and backpedaled several steps. His hand closed over air, and his jaw set. Annoyance flashed in his eyes.

"I— Sorry." Dell skidded to a halt, eyes wide as she panned from him to me. "Miguel's got a fix on the kelpie."

The gold in his eyes simmered. "Where?"

"It's in a cave system beneath the lake." Specks of dirt on her tennis shoes commanded her sudden interest. "Our patrols must have corralled it."

"We drove it into the water," he said under his breath as though that outcome unsettled him.

Why hadn't it escaped when it had the chance? The absence of a scent trail meant the wargs had no way of tracking it. Why had it approached us in the first place? Why parade its prey in front of us? The thing was inciting us to action, and that kind of boldness made me nervous. "The girl couldn't have survived this long in the water."

"Unless that's what he does," Graeson said, shifting uneasily. "We don't know how he picks his locations. I'm not sure about the other sites, but I know there is a cavern beneath the lake where—" his voice hitched, "—Marie was found. A water sprite lived there when I was a boy. She used to talk to me when I was hunting in wolf form."

The way he said it made me curious. "Does she still live there?" Some fae hibernated for decades at a time.

"No. She was accused a drowning a young man she favored. Some said they were lovers. I think she was beautiful and he was tempted by her. If she harmed him, then she was protecting herself." His expression soured. "The conclave swept in and removed her before Bessemer got it in his head to sanction a hunt without a trial. Now her name will never be cleared, and she won't be allowed to return home for as long as Bessemer lives. That type of fae…" Old sadness rang out. "They bond to their homes. Relocating her was a death sentence."

That might explain his distrust for the conclave. They had hurt a friend of his. His fondness for the sprite might also explain why he had greeted me with an open mind instead of the prejudice so many wargs held against fae.

"You think this might be part of his pattern." I turned the idea over in my head. "We know he keeps his victims alive for a week or longer. If he's choosing bodies of water with fae-created cave systems, then there may be dry caverns and oxygen too."

"The kelpie could stash its victim there until the time was right," Graeson agreed.

"How do we find out what's underneath this lake without tapping into conclave resources?" Without Internet access, we couldn't Google geography or touch base with my contacts. "Local fae would know. I'm going to need that ride into town now."

"No." Graeson rubbed his chin. "You won't. I have someone in mind."

"Who? Last I checked, wargs don't have gills." I crossed to Dell and touched her shoulder. She peered up at me through fringe bangs. "We have to call Vause." We had no choice. "It would take days to assemble a dive team capable of handling the kelpie without asking the conclave for assistance. This victim doesn't have that kind of time."

"There's another option, a safer choice."

On reflex, my hand clamped over the pearl bracelet on my opposite wrist as though protecting it might shield Harlow too. "Harlow isn't well enough to go up against a kelpie."

A mermaid would have made me hesitate, but a human? She didn't stand a chance.

He didn't miss a beat. "Medics cleared her this morning."

"How do you—?" With sinking certainty I knew. "You've been keeping tabs on her in case you needed her."

The announcement shouldn't have surprised me. Graeson was all about protecting his resources.

Maybe I had done wrong by going along with his plan. It seemed he and Vause were surfing the same wavelength after all.

"Harlow is facing suspension. She'll be sidelined until an internal affairs investigation finishes with her, and we both know it's a formality. She lied on her application. They aren't going to forgive or forget that. She'll be lucky if they don't press charges." His gaze dipped in a rare show of deference. "I offered to hire her, and she accepted. I didn't push her into this."

"You didn't have to," I stated the obvious. "What options does she have?"

All those clothes and hair products didn't come cheap. I might not be a girly girl, but as often as I traveled, I had gotten lost in my share of superstore aisles and gaped at the seven dollar tubes of lipstick and ten dollar tubes of foundation. It cost a fortune to wear enough cosmetics that it appeared you wore none. Faced with a crimp in her income, of course Harlow would jump at the chance to earn fast cash.

"I put her up at a hotel in town." He chose to regard my question as rhetorical. "I'll send someone to pick her up when we're ready."

Disappointment sapped the fight out of me. "You think of everything, don't you?"

His jaw flexed. "Someone has to."

Graeson set off toward the shack at a clipped pace, and I watched him go. Dell shrank into herself, and it frayed my last nerve.

"He doesn't care what it costs the rest of us as long as he gets what he wants." The kelpie had to be brought down, but I was afraid Harlow would take the fall. "Does he have a conscience at all?"

"That's what I was trying to tell you earlier," she said softly. "He gave his grief to the pack."

"Gave it away? That's something a warg can just hand over?" Her gaze darted from left to right before she nodded, and my stomach cramped. "As in he no longer feels it?"

"We took it and spread it out among ourselves. That's why he's in my head. The pack bond is always present, but usually it's muted to give us all our privacy. Cord has to keep his mind wide open so we can sort of... It's hard to explain. It's like siphoning the negative energy. Right now he's an open book, and your name is scribbled on a lot of pages."

A flush spread up my nape. "How long will it last?"

"A few days, maybe a week. That's why he's pushing so hard. He's running out of time. The grief was eating his mind. He couldn't think for replaying the last time he saw Marie. They fought over something stupid. She wanted to go to the movies with a boy, and he said no. She yelled hurtful things, stormed off to her best friend's house then didn't come home. He blames himself for what happened." Her voice wavered. "He's our beta. Her death happened on Chandler pack land. It's his duty—as second to Bessemer and as her brother—to find her killer and punish him. If Cord doesn't deliver before the next full moon, then the first order of business will be an open challenge on him for his position, and Cord is too dominant to let that happen. He'll fight to the death before he's demoted. It's instinct."

I spat a string of curses. "What kind of leader throws his own people to the wolves?" Literally.

Wargs valued strength, both physical and emotional. I got that. They were all about survival of the fittest. I got that too. But the man had lost his sister. And his alpha, who should have been sympathetic, had set Graeson on the kelpie's trail with an ultimatum. No wonder he was bending all the rules. This was about more than Marie. It was about the rest of his life, his position within the pack. He was fighting for her memory as well as his own future.

"Come on." I grabbed Dell by the hand and dragged her toward the shack. "I need to have a chat with Mr. Machination about the rules before Harlow gets here."

Damn Graeson for his scheming. As furious as I was on Harlow's behalf, I couldn't walk away now. I was in too deep. There was a sliver of a chance Roni might still be alive. That was enough to keep me in line, and Graeson knew it. But that didn't mean I was going to let him sacrifice us all in the name of revenge. As much as my palms itched to strangle him, one day his grief would rebound, and that was punishment enough as far as I was concerned.

Harlow arrived ten minutes after I retreated up the rickety stairs to my temporary quarters. Dell sat on the cot while I paced the room from end to end, which is to say I took five steps before I had to turn in order to take five more. The familiar ping of gravel bouncing off undercarriage drew me to the window.

The younger witchy brother opened the rear passenger door of the SUV and offered Harlow his hand with a flourish of harmless gallantry that tempted my eyes toward the ceiling. She blushed prettily and allowed him to help her hop onto the ground.

Tonight she wore her candy-bright hair in a French braid that complemented her Creamsicle orange tank top and tie-dyed postage-stamp-sized shorts. Even the straps on her wedge sandals matched. Factor in the serviceable brown leather bag she wore like a backpack, and the bright colors made her appear even younger, more innocent. The ball of anxiety in my gut tightened when she spotted me and waved with so much enthusiasm she wobbled in the gravel. The witch had to steady her by wrapping his arm around her waist.

"They're here," I said more for myself than for Dell. With her hearing, she had probably tracked their impending arrival for several minutes. I blew out a breath and took the stairs at a clip. Two wargs were out on patrol. Two more stood on the porch. Another pair flanked Graeson, who occupied the center of the room with a clear view of the vehicle through the window. Miguel waited at the register with a bland expression, as if only his brother knew the secret to drawing out his fiery temper.

The witch led Harlow up the steps and held the door for her. She spotted me, scuffed her shoe on the planks once then shuffled up to me. She slid her arms around my waist in a fragile hug I didn't expect. I went tense, and she felt ready to break apart in my arms. The shock faded when her shoulders hitched in what I feared was a quiet sob, and I squeezed her back with everything I had.

She didn't thank me this time. The watery film covering her eyes when she looked at me did it for her.

"How are you feeling?" I summoned the brightest smile in my repertoire, the Aunt Dot Special, the one I flashed when I got home from a long trip and she was waiting on my porch to welcome me with a kiss to my forehead and a hug that smelled of her homemade rose perfume.

"The medics waved their magic wands over me." She pulled back, and her fingers brushed her cheek dry. "They healed me before I had a chance to scar. It's amazing what magic can accomplish these days."

Though she had just climbed the steps, I led her back out again. Warg hearing being what it was, we couldn't venture far enough for true privacy, but at least I wouldn't have to see them hanging on my every word and zapping mental commentary back and forth among themselves.

"What happened at the Rebec place—" I began.

"It's okay. Really." A wavy strand of her hair had come undone, and she wrapped it around her finger. "You did what you had to do. You saved me. Again." She tugged on the curl. "I think you managed what Mom failed to do. You knocked some sense into me. I see now that I don't belong here. On land, I mean. I thought it would be… But it isn't. Guess I'm more fish than girl." A tired exhale. "I've made it this far. Graeson is paying me out of pocket for this gig, and that's money I need for the trip." She glanced up. "I'm going to stick around until Charybdis is captured. After that I'm heading home. For good."

A pang arrowed through me. If Harlow returned to the sea, our paths would never cross again. Lakes were bad enough. An ocean? No. That was asking too much. I couldn't face open water. Given Harlow's experience topside with rage-mongering fae, I could hardly blame her for choosing the sea over land. Even if the water was no less dangerous, it was a familiar threat to her. "Are you sure you're up for this?"

"I'm tougher than I look." Harlow squared her shoulders. "I can do this."

"The kelpie is still down there." Or so the witches claimed. "Can you fend him off alone?"

"I can swim circles around him." A smile touched her lips. "I'm a mermaid, remember?"

An all-too-human one.

Hinges groaned behind us, and I turned as Graeson stepped onto the porch. The wargs hovered behind him. "We don't have much time," he announced. "The Garzas' latest divination places the kelpie in Butler, Tennessee this time next week."

A prickle of unease lifted hairs down my arms. I didn't want Charybdis in the same state as my family.

"I'm ready when you are." Harlow tugged on the strap of her backpack. "I've got everything I need right here."

The beta looked at me with fierce, shining eyes when he said, "This ends tonight."

I hoped he was right.

CHAPTER FIFTEEN

Sardis Lake reflected the moon in its belly. Insects skating over the surface of the water caused ripples as their slender legs glided. I stood at the base of the pier where the Tanner sisters had gone fishing, the closest I had come to this particular site. A knocking sound made me frown. I scanned the night for its source while praying it wasn't my knees.

"It's not too late to call in the conclave," I murmured, wary of fuzzy ears picking up the offer.

Somewhere wolves prowled the woods on soft paws. Harlow's one sticking point was she wanted complete privacy for her "change". I got a pass, because I knew her secret. That and she had been shivering since we left. Even in the dark, the temperature hung in the mid-eighties. Cold wasn't to blame for her teeth chattering.

"I've got this. Don't worry so much." Harlow dropped her bag on the planks, adjusted her skintight neoprene top, this one in black, and sat. "You look ready to yak. Are you sure *you* can handle this?"

"No." I backed up until the heels of my boots sank deep into the sandy soil. "I'm not."

My honesty must have shaken her, because her fingers slipped on the lock fastened to an inner pocket. "We're not alone." I got the feeling she was comforting herself. "We've got the wolves for backup." She wiped her hands and tried again. "That's what—eight wargs? They can swim, right?"

"As far as I know." The smell of wet dog almost bowled me over whenever I entered the shack. "I don't see Graeson making his stand here if the pack wasn't willing to get their paws wet."

"Yeah. You're probably right." After that ringing endorsement, she let her eyes go unfocused while she gazed across the water. "There are no naturally occurring aquatic caves in the area. Whatever's down there was hand carved. The Mississippi River is maybe an hour away. Freshies use it like a highway. It's not impossible that a large body of water like this one, so close to a main 'road', might be used as nesting grounds." Her voice went soft. "There could be caves for miles down there depending on the size of the pod."

"Freshies are freshwater mermaids?" I clarified.

"Yes." Her eyebrows lifted. "Salties—like my parents—view them as hillbilly cousins or something. *Lots* of animosity there."

Thierry hadn't said one way or the other, but the mermaids in Wink must be freshies to live so far inland. That might explain why Harlow's attempts to soothe the kraken backfired. If it shared its masters' hatred for salties, then it wouldn't hesitate to attack an enemy invading a potential nesting ground. Going in a human and a saltie? Harlow never stood a chance. She should have bowed out once she realized how long her odds were, but she hadn't. Youth tended to give us all the illusion of invincibility.

"What are the odds of us recovering—" I almost slipped and said *a body*, "—Roni?"

"Warrens are difficult to navigate even when you're familiar with them. Scent markers are the only way to be sure of where you're going, so keep your fingers crossed that it's been a while since a pod used the lake." She opened a jar and removed a glob of flesh-colored goo. "The fewer smells competing for my attention, the easier it will be to lock on to where the kelpie is hiding."

I wrinkled my nose when she liberally applied the gel to the sides of her throat. "What are you doing?"

When Harlow removed her hand, pink-rimmed gills flexed from her collarbone to under her ears. "A girl's gotta breathe, right? It takes a few minutes for them to become fully functional." Next she removed a dagger with a shell-encrusted handle and tucked it into a pouch sewn into her top. Gingerly she eased out what appeared to be a pair of black yoga shorts from her pack. Instead of standing upright to change, she laid back on the planks, wiggling her hips to pull the stretchy fabric on over the pair she already wore. "If you like that..." she huffed, "...you'll love my next trick."

I waited. Nothing happened. "Should I clap?"

"Give me a second." She scooched over to the edge, dipped her hand in the lake and poured water onto her lap. Golden scales with a rosy hue glimmered where each drop fell. "The real magic happens in the water." She rolled hard to her left. "Be right back."

Splash.

Her tail breached seconds later, and her head popped up five minutes after that. Streaming water, she was radiant.

I gaped after her. I owed her applause after all.

"How is this possible?" Magic was capable of many things, but giving a girl reusable fins and gills? "Can all initiates do this?"

What I meant was—did the same change that allowed the merfolk to walk on land for a year also cause a false positive? Maybe Harlow wasn't human. Maybe if I touched her now, while she wore her tail, I would read her differently. As long as I had puzzled over her mystery, I couldn't stem my curiosity. Being stumped by a classification for the first time had been driving me nuts.

"I'm a changeling." She bobbed in the water. "The human half of the equation, obviously."

So much for that theory.

"That explains the texture of the magic in your aura." The sensation was so slight even charismatic humans registered in her range. "At first I thought it meant you were a witch, but the signature was too faint."

"No hocus-pocus here. Well, none generated by me." She returned to the dock, dragged her bag closer and removed two small discs I recognized as rudimentary healing spells. She jiggled the pouches to settle their contents then tucked them into her top before snapping and knotting the various closures. She spoke to the fabric as if telling it her story was easier than facing me. "My parents made the arrangements for me."

"Your parents." Human or mermaid or both, I wondered.

"Both merfolk," she answered my unspoken question. "I'm the only human in the pod."

"How did you manage that?" I asked, half joking. Changelings were usually compatible on a base level with their adoptive parents. Dropping a human infant into the sea and expecting it to survive among merfolk stretched that definition.

"My mother is cursed. All of her children die the hour they turn six weeks old. Sixteen years ago my father was so distraught at her pain, he made a bargain with a brownie who cleaned and mended for a human family with thirteen children. They couldn't afford another mouth to feed, and the brownie made sure they didn't have one for long. The humans had been praying for a miracle, and the brownie overheard them and granted one."

"The brownie swapped you for the merchild," I supplied.

"Yes." She secured the backpack to one of the pilings, and when the fabric got damp, a cluster of chalky-white bay barnacles burst over the surface, the kind you'd expect to see on the belly of a freighter. Glamour perhaps? "When the infant died, my father left my birth parents my weight in gold and precious gems. They were compensated for their loss, as much as any mortal is among the fae, and Mom got what she had always wanted." She pointed both of her thumbs at her chest.

If she expected condemnation from me, she would be waiting a long time. Fae traditions were older than the ground under my feet. The rights and wrongs of fae and men were not mine to judge.

"The Rumspringa thing I told you about…" She blushed. "It's pretty much a total lie. Sorry. Telling the story was habit by the time I met you."

I waved off her apology. "Your parents were wise to give you a chance to see how humans and fae live topside together." Otherwise she would have always been curious about the wonders of land, maybe even grown to resent her mother and father for not having a chance to embrace both sides of her heritage. "I do have one more question. Why do you wear the tail sometimes and not others? It seems like it would give you an advantage."

"The magic requires time to regenerate. It's not an issue at home, in salt water, but here it's difficult to recharge that specific type of magic." A dismissive shrug. "Not so much a mystery as a practicality."

I mulled over her answer, imagining her soaking the shorts in a salt bath in her hotel room to rejuvenate them, and found the whimsy of Harlow's life enchanting. "I hope you're happy with your choice."

“That makes two of us.” A tight smile stretched her lips. “Well.” The barnacles’ cling was tested by Harlow twisting the bag until it faced under the dock. “I’m ready. How about you?”

“I hate that you have to go alone.”

“I’ve survived worse odds.” She knocked on the warped planks. “Besides, you’re here.” She drifted away from the dock. “You won’t let anything happen to me.”

The pearl bracelet felt tight around my wrist. I ran my finger underneath to loosen it.

With a flip of her tail, Harlow vanished beneath the surface, and the waiting game began.

CHAPTER SIXTEEN

Ten minutes passed counted out by my fingers tapping against my thigh. *Ten.* Some humans could hold their breath for twenty-odd minutes. The record was something like twenty-two minutes and twenty-two seconds. Nonaquatic fae had a similar lung capacity. That said, the average human only managed thirty or forty seconds before they started gasping for air.

Not that I was obsessed with drowning statistics or anything, but how would a nine-year-old girl survive such an arduous trip to the surface? If she was still alive at all. Harlow might be fast, but if the caves ran as deep as she thought they might, then pressure sickness might also be a factor. Too many variables. Too many grim thoughts circling me. I was sick of them.

"Is it safe to come out now?"

The sound of Dell's voice eased the tension in my shoulders. "I didn't hear you."

"You weren't supposed to." Her next steps made enough noise to compensate for the previous ones. Moonlight glimmered in her hair and bathed her cheeks when she winked at me. "Stealth mode and all that."

"The patrols haven't turned up anything?"

"Nothing so far." She tapped the side of her nose. "The scent from the parking lot was strong enough we all imprinted a scent memory. We'll know the creature if we come across it again."

"That's good news." As fast as news traveled among the wargs, having Dell with me was as good as wearing a headset and listening in to comm chatter. Or it would be if she heard the pack bond as well in human form as she did as a wolf. "Is everyone in place?"

"The lake is surrounded," she assured me. "It can't get on land without one of us seeing or hearing it, even if it casts again and we lose the scent."

A pack of wargs could handle the kelpie if Harlow spooked it. I was more worried about what was happening under the water. The question of *what is Charybdis* hadn't been answered to my satisfaction yet either. Were we dealing with one fae? Or two who shared a magical signature?

If a practitioner put in an appearance, we weren't without resources. We had two witches on our side, but Charybdis was fae or at least from Faerie. His magic would be fae magic. The Garzas cast earth magic. Even with a home-field advantage, the Garzas might not stack up against the mystery fae.

"We could ask the Garzas to cast again," Dell was saying, "but by the time they finished, this op will be over."

A bloodcurdling scream glazed my spine with fear. The ethereal white head of a delicately boned horse parted the surface of the water. Steam bellowed from its nostrils. Its mane rippled in the still night air as though the strands were as dry as bone. Hooves stamped the water in front of it, and a massive tail whipped the water in its wake.

"Fish sticks," Dell cursed. "I need to shift. I have to warn the others."

An enormous silvery gray wolf with white markings on its forelegs kicked up dirt when it landed beside me. Its teeth were bared, and drool hung from its muzzle. I stumbled into Dell before my brain caught up to my feet. "Graeson?" The wolf's hazel eyes flicked to me, and a sarcastic wag moved his tail before he lowered his shoulders and snarled at the stampeding kelpie. "You can't take on a kelpie alone."

The wolf, who must have been hiding in the trees all along, ignored me.

Dell cocked her head, already listening to things beyond my perception while her bones cracked and the change took her. "The others…will be here…soon."

A vicious shriek pierced my ears. The kelpie was gaining speed, and I was a sitting duck without borrowed magic to wield. We had expected the kelpie to flee. We figured it would exit the far end of the lake, the farthest point from civilization. It must have followed

Harlow's scent trail back to the pier. It wanted this confrontation. It came looking for a fight.

"I can't stand back and watch you two fight this thing." I stuck out my hand. "Please, Dell. Let me help you."

Understanding tensed her shoulders, but she clasped hands with me. "Don't die. I'll get in so much trouble if you kick the bucket."

Fingers damp in her grip, I timed it so my spur pierced Dell's palm the moment the kelpie's front hooves struck sand. A bestial cry rang out as it hauled itself forward in graceless increments. Its tail flipped and kicked up dirt until a burst of white magic dissolved the giant fins into muscular rear legs. With all four legs under it, the kelpie charged.

Tawny fur rippled down my arm the instant the tang of Dell's blood registered in the back of my throat. Straining, I focused on the burn of magic, directed it, and slowly the nails on my other hand blackened and lengthened to razor tips.

Jaws wide, the gray wolf at my side lunged for the kelpie's throat. Popping noises and soft whimpers told me Dell was mid-change. I circled around the kelpie, claws flexing, waiting for an opening. Graeson slung his head back and forth, ripping flesh and exposing the beast's windpipe. His nails dug into its fur and gave him leverage to clamp his jaws deeper in the delicate skin.

The scent of raw meat made my stomach rumble. Must be the wolf blood, because I was a well-done kind of girl.

Graeson's assault left no room for me. The hindquarters were too dangerous. The front end wasn't much better. The throat was its weakest point, and the warg necklace the kelpie wore was stripping tendon to the bone.

A groan turned growl preceded the golden wolf who positioned herself between the fight and me. Head low and tail dragging the ground, Dell rumbled in her throat. The motion drew the kelpie's eye, and its slimy gaze raked over me. The beast trumpeted a shrill whinny. Its black pupils expanded until only crystalline voids remained where its eyes had been. Their emptiness sucked at the edge of my consciousness, lured me forward and made my palms itch with the need to caress the kelpie's silky hide, to run my fingers through its flowing hair. For a moment, the world spun in orbit around me, and the unforgiving fabric of the universe spread as far as my eyes could see. There was peace in death, and the creature offered it to me. Its vision enveloped me, and the surcease of pain was such a welcome relief that my bones melted with promise.

In the distance, miles away, light-years from me, the sounds of Graeson's feasting rent the air. Another sound, a whine accompanied by the insistent nudging of a furry head against my thigh, yanked me from the kelpie's trap, and I gasped as the world rushed back into focus.

A nicker passed the kelpie's lips before it twisted, slinging Graeson off his feet. Graeson hung on by the tips of his fangs. When the horse let him touch down, it nailed him in the stomach with the sharp edge of a front hoof. Blood slicked his fur. He was hurt. Badly.

Seeing its opening, the kelpie stomped on Graeson's tail and reared back its head, shredding its own throat as it tried ripping the warg off. Its feet stamped, eager for the chance to crush the wolf beneath them. It was my cue. I couldn't wait another second. I rushed forward with Dell bounding two strides ahead of me.

The beast rotated its torso to the right, and Graeson slung free, his body splashing into the water. It spotted Dell and pivoted on its front feet, bucking wildly and clipping her on the chin with its rear leg. Her head snapped back. She hit the water and didn't move. I ran to haul them out before they drowned.

"A little help would be nice," I yelled to the wargs who had yet to materialize.

I bolted for Dell, but the kelpie cut me off. It didn't charge. It didn't move. Maybe it couldn't now that it had expended so much energy on attacking the wargs. It stared me down while its life drained away in bluish fluids that slicked its chest. I didn't have time to waste. Already prickles raced up my arms. Splitting the magic across two limbs was costing me. I swung my arm and raked furrows across the kelpie's snout. It reared on its hind legs and screamed. I swung again, swiping its chest. It planted its front feet and whirled its hind legs. When it kicked out, air whistled over my head, but I ducked under its vicious hooves. I wasn't fast enough to dodge its second strike, and the next thing I knew I was flying.

I hit the water. Hard. I gritted my teeth and gasped as the warm liquid closed over my head and the sound of my frantic pulse hammered in my ears. My body sank fast and so far, I thought I would never stop dropping. My frantic mind conjured Lori floating beside me, hand extended, encouraging me to let her guide me into the deeps where she had gone.

The bitter tang of fear and blood filled my mouth, and a second, more desperate change swept over me as Lori waited out my oxygen with an eager smile curving her lips. It was as if the wavering apparition had possessed me, ready to relive her death. The arms grasping for the surface were now slender and pale. My hands were small, and a kitten bandage covered one of my knuckles.

Childish laughter tinkled in my ears. The sea boiled and frothed. Waves pelted me, sucked my feet from under me. My back hit the sand. My ears rang. Water rose up my chest, fizzled over my neck until it crested over my head. One heartbeat, two. It retreated in a dizzying rush, nursed my toes and tried to draw me out to sea with it. Salt made my face sticky. Tears or ocean water, I wasn't sure.

A thick arm wrapped around my waist, and I cried out as reality splintered the memory. The remaining air in my lungs expelled from the pressure. I blinked through murky waters and found Graeson's human face inches from mine. His eyes glowed in the low light, wild and furious.

I clawed at my throat, couldn't breathe. So much water. In my eyes, my nose, my ears. Crushing me. Graeson was strong, but he was injured, one leg shattered by the kelpie. He struggled to haul us both to the surface.

Lori's pale hands fisted his shirt. The gods weren't so cruel as to let her die the same way twice, were they? Hadn't I been punished enough? Or did I have to follow in her footsteps as I should have done that night so long ago?

Graeson scissored his legs and pinned me to him with one arm while he swam with the other. Pressure lessened. The pain banding my chest became bearable. Our heads burst from the water, and I gasped and choked until my throat burned. I shivered so hard my teeth chattered even though the water was as warm as the last shower I had taken.

"Hold on," he panted. "I've got you."

I clung to him, wrapping my legs around his waist and my arms around his neck until he made a gurgling noise. He twisted in the water so I rode astride his chest as he paddled backward toward the shore. In a day or two I would be mortified. Right now I was too damn grateful to be alive. I propped my chin on my shoulder to keep my face out of the water. Graeson's nose barely breached the surface, but his heart thumped steady against my chest.

Helping hands hauled us ashore next to the partially devoured kelpie corpse. The pack must have finished it off while Graeson shifted and came after me. "Bring us a blanket," he ground out between his teeth, pain lowering his voice a register.

I ought to let go. Supporting my weight had to have been agony for Graeson with his busted leg, but I couldn't release him. My muscles were locked. He was a safe harbor, and I wanted so much to remain in the shelter of his arms.

"Is that the Tanner girl?" One of the wargs opened his arms to receive me. "It's all right, darlin'. I won't hurt you."

Graeson's snarl reverberated through my bones. *"Mine."*

The warg's expression slipped, confusion knitting his brow until he leaned forward and inhaled. His eyes widened in recognition. "Agent Ellis." The sound of my name ramped up Graeson's anger. The warg held his hands up, palms out, and started walking backward until the beta calmed. "Call if you need anything." He was looking at Graeson when he said it, not in the eyes, but at chest level, a height that wouldn't instigate a challenge for dominance, but a wary inflection in his voice convinced me he was talking to me.

"Leave us," Graeson grumbled then turned on his heel, not waiting to see if the other warg obeyed him, before walking into the shelter of the pines where he sat with me on his lap. Unseen hands wrapped a blanket around my shoulders. Stuck flush to him as I was, it made a heavy cocoon for us.

I rested my face against his neck, each breath drawing in the comforting scent of his skin. As my nerves calmed, prickles coasted down my limbs. His arms held me tight while my body juddered, and I lost my grip on Lori. Panting through the cocktail of panic, fear and hurt, I swallowed hard and pushed against his chest.

"I should..." Stand up, walk away, ask questions, anything but sit there and let him hold me like he cared I had almost died. The kelpie was dead. I had to touch the beast to confirm the magical signature before the wargs polished off the corpse. I shoved away from him, toes brushing the ground, but then Dell was there, and she put her hand on my shoulder.

"Stay." The pressure of her fingers was enough to coax me back against Graeson. "His wolf needs to accept you're safe." His arms eased when I complied. Dell patted me. "Give Cord a minute to rein him in."

Her warning drew my gaze upward. His eyes shined like golden beacons, with all the warmth of lighthouse torches. Now that I was myself again, his nose buried against my throat, under my ear, putting his teeth close to my pulse. I swallowed and let him drag my scent deep into his lungs. A long time later, his grip loosened enough for me to clamber off his lap.

Dell offered me a hand up and inched between us when Graeson growled like she had stolen a raw New York strip out of his food bowl. "Cam is not pack." Her voice trembled. "You can't hold her if she doesn't want to be held."

"Mine," he warned her in a voice that was more beast than man.

"No," Dell told him, stronger this time.

Graeson looked over as if leaving the matter up to me to decide. I kept my mouth shut. I didn't want to risk sticking my foot in it. He had claimed me when the Fury threatened my life. I fought him then, and it had done no good. His wolf wasn't a fan of the word *no*. He had been protecting me from Letitia at the time, so I didn't take the possessiveness too seriously. I was weaker than a warg, and Graeson's inner beast was the next best thing to an alpha. Protecting those weaker than himself was instinct. It wasn't personal. It was reflex.

"You should rest," I said instead of any of the dozens of things whirling through my head.

The light went out of Graeson's eyes, and he waved at us in dismissal. He bent his knees and let his head fall back against the tree trunk. He stared at the sky through the pine needles while a scowl cut his mouth.

With a fleeting smile meant to reassure, Dell wrung water from her hair. "Maybe you shouldn't shift again around Cord."

The weight of his disappointment chased me out of the trees. “Maybe you’re right.”

CHAPTER SEVENTEEN

I don't know how long I stood there, feet planted on the first plank of the dock, staring at the water until my eyes dried out and blinking hurt. The kelpie was dead. Its circle would never set. I had touched its hoof and confirmed its magical signature as the one present at all the crime scenes. We had stopped it from doing whatever it had meant to do. The thought didn't comfort. So many young lives had been lost for nothing. And now two more hung in the balance.

The skin where my shirt had dried itched, so I scratched my elbow. "How long has Harlow been down there?"

The sky had lightened, but the moon hung overhead as if unwilling to break its vigil. How long had the scuffle lasted? Five minutes? Ten? How long had it taken Graeson to haul Dell and then me out of the water? It was impossible to guess. At the time, terror had stretched each of those seconds into hours.

"Three hours all told is my guess." Dell stood so our shoulders almost touched. "You said she thought there might be caves down there?"

"Yes," I said for the dozenth time.

A note of forced cheer entered her voice. "Then three hours isn't all that long."

"No." I sounded hollow. "It isn't."

A long howl rolled across the water. It was picked up and carried around the perimeter of the lake until it reached us. Dell clamped a hand on my arm, her face splotchy from concentration as she deciphered the howls. "Three black SUVs have been spotted on the road leading to the campground."

"The conclave." A jittery feeling took root in my chest. "How are we going to play this?"

Rolling up on a dead kelpie gnawed to bits meant I couldn't cover for Graeson or hide the pack's involvement. The conclave would demand answers, they would expect me to run into their arms, and we had to give them what they wanted in order to keep the peace between species.

"We're pulling out." Graeson's voice came from behind me. "You're coming with us."

"I can't run from them, or they'll think I'm complicit." I didn't turn to look at him. Our moment under the pines lingered too fresh in my mind. I didn't want to disappoint him again, which made no sense when his desire to use me was a perpetual disappointment to me. "I'll lose my job."

"Your job?" His bare feet slapped the compacted dirt. "Leaving with us, finding who wiped the scenes for the kelpie, that's your job." His voice came from right behind me. "Don't you see? Charybdis sacrificed his pawn. We were too close. He gave the kelpie to us. He paraded it around the shack where we were staying to make damn sure we took the bait. He sent it back into that lake when he could have saved it to buy himself time to escape. He knew about the divinations, or he guessed we used a tracking spell to get in front of him. He knew we would dig in and find the kelpie and kill it." He drew a ragged breath. "He wants the conclave's Charybdis file closed. He wants a fresh start, because now he has to find a new way to accomplish his goals. We can't stop now. Not when we're so close."

"I can't leave Harlow." I couldn't tear my gaze from the water hoping she would appear. "She could be injured. If I'm not here when—"

"—*if*," he corrected me, and I hated him a little for it. "The conclave will be here in fifteen minutes." A hard note entered his voice. "Twenty if they check the other sites or hit the shack first."

I rolled a shoulder. "Then you better go if you want to get a head start."

"This isn't over." He grabbed my arm and swung me to face him. "You know there's more to this."

More to the deaths? Or more to him and me? The molten heat in his gaze caused my neurons to misfire.

"Don't try to misunderstand me. You want to pretend there's nothing between us, but damn it, Ellis, I can't just let you go." He shook me. "Not when my every instinct is telling me you belong to me."

"You can't believe that, and I certainly don't." A sad laugh forced its way clear of my throat. "You kidnapped me. You earmarked me to use as bait. You took my deepest hurt and twisted it for your own use."

"I fucked up, all right? Is that what you want to hear?" A growl entered his voice. "Yes, I drove you up here without your consent. Yes, I planned on using you as bait, but I didn't, did I?"

"No thanks to you," I growled right back. "The Garzas found him."

"Who do you think called them here? Who do you think begged for their help? Do you think a couple of witches wanted to hang out in a bait shack with eight wolves for a long weekend? Do you know how much they cost me?"

"They're your family," I started.

"They're also coven witches. They don't work for free. Not even for blood." He searched my face. "I had to pay them, because their priest expects a cut for their services. They're the best, and they command a high price."

"Your sister deserved the best," I said numbly, disbelieving.

"Marie is dead." His voice broke. "I couldn't save her." Desperation touched his eyes. "I did this for *you*."

My heart skipped a beat. "They had no way of knowing he had already chosen a victim. If he hadn't—"

"Then I would have found another way." He cupped my face in his hands. "I'm messed up, Ellis. I know that. You know that. I didn't expect to meet you. Not here. Not now. But I did, and I won't let you go so easily."

My resolve wavered. This thing with Charybdis was far from over. The kelpie had a partner, and he was still out there. Did I trust the conclave to finish the hunt? It was a hard question to answer when I had believed in their mission to help faekind enough to join their ranks. I was a Gemini first. Now the oath I had given rang hollow in my memory. There were layers to this case as yet unsolved, and handing the evidence over to the conclave meant accepting the possibility they might close the case and sweep their involvement under the rug. Graeson would yank the metaphorical broom from their hands and snap the handle. He and I would sift through the dust bunnies until every grain of truth was documented and the people responsible were disposed of like so much trash.

Was that what I wanted? Was *he* what I wanted?

"Uh, guys." Dell hooked my arm and whirled me back toward the lake. "Do you see that?"

Being tugged between two wargs like a juicy bone left my eyes rattling in my skull. "What am I looking for?"

Dell pointed where a sheet of white fabric billowed across the gently bobbing waters, a stark contrast to the bleak depths of the lake. Bubbles popped and fizzled around its ragged edges as if it had been propelled to the surface and might sink again once the oxygen saturating it dissipated.

Taking the opportunity to step away from Graeson, I walked until the water licked the toes of my boots and gritted my teeth to keep the past at bay.

He grasped my wrist and held tight, a reminder our conversation wasn't finished. "Is that...?" He snapped his fingers at the wargs closest to us. "Boots off. I want whatever that is retrieved."

The female warg hit the water. She stalled out mid-stroke when she got near enough to touch the opaque spot. "It's just cloth." She lifted it over her head then let it slap the surface.

My head fell back on my neck. I searched the sky for signs, for hope, but it was as cruel in its indifference as always.

A wet explosion jerked my head forward as a massive sphere jettisoned into the air, clearing the water by several feet before it dropped like a stone, slapping the surface and settling in to rock on the waves its eruption had caused. Two figures huddled in its center, one curled in the bottom while the other sat upright. I glimpsed bright pink hair splayed beneath the resting figure, and my heart soared.

"It's Harlow." I wriggled away from Graeson and ran down the dock to its end. The murky depths below spun vertigo in my ears, and I wobbled, but I managed to stay on my feet. I cupped my hands around my mouth and called to the warg, "She's with us. Bring her in."

The female hesitated until Graeson threw his weight behind the order. "You heard her. Get them to dry land."

Two more males dove into the water. The female circled the bubble while smoothing her hands along its sides. Whatever type of magic had constructed it, it was solid. Together the wargs rolled the bubble safely to the shore. I ran back toward them and leapt, meeting the soaked wargs in the damp sand. Inside the strange sphere a petite girl sat with her legs crossed. She wore a pair of blue panties, a matching training bra and one sock. Harlow curved around her, her head resting on the girl's tiny lap while she stroked the pink strands as though soothing them both.

Relief wilted the girl when she spotted the mutilated kelpie. Tears sprang to her eyes, and her protective grip tightened on Harlow.

"Roni," I said, voice thick with emotion.

The girl's head jerked toward me. "Who are you?"

"I'm Camille Ellis. I work with the Earthen Conclave." When that got me nowhere, I tacked on, "I'm Harlow's friend." I showed Roni my empty hands, hoping to convince her I meant no harm, but she cast me a shrewd look that said she knew sometimes the worst dangers were the unseen ones. Considering she had gotten into this situation by having a tender heart, I understood her hesitance to trust me. "You're safe now. See those lights?" I pointed through the trees to the partially concealed road. "Once those cars get here, we'll find you a phone and let you call your mom and sister, okay? They can meet us at the nearest hospital, and we'll get you checked out."

Or failing that, the nearest safe house with a fae medic on staff. Roni hadn't been missing long, but she must be starving. Elizabeth McKenna escaped with her life but not without injury. I hadn't been greedy then, and I wouldn't be now. Roni was alive. That was all that mattered.

"You know Daphne?" Roni's bottom lip trembled. "Is she mad at me?"

"No." I sank to one knee and put my face at her level. "She's worried sick about you. Your mom is too." I touched the bubble's spongy surface. "Did you make this? What is it?"

A sharp nod. "It's just air magic."

"That's a very neat trick," I praised her. "Maybe sometime you can show me how it works."

A slower nod, one I could tell she didn't mean but did all the same to be polite.

"I need you to let me in, Roni." I touched the wall where Harlow's head rested. "My friend doesn't look well. She needs a doctor too."

"I—I can't." Tears rolled down Roni's cheeks to splash on Harlow's chin as she slung her head from side to side. "The bubble happens when I get scared." She trembled. "It won't go away. I'm trying, but I'm stuck."

Motion in the corner of my eye left me gritting my teeth. "Stand back." I shooed the wargs away from us. They wanted to help, but half of them were still wolves, and it was obvious Roni wasn't ready to deal with more animals. Eyes as wide as dinner plates, she was too frightened. "Go someplace and shift, or stick to the trees."

The pack obeyed me without question, which appeared to please Graeson, and that worried me. Anything making him happy made me nervous. Being accepted by his pack, even for the night, felt like I had walked into a trap he was attempting to close behind me.

"What if we try talking first?" All I needed was for Roni to shift her focus enough that her magic weakened, then we could pull Harlow onto land and evaluate the extent of her injuries. "Can you tell me what happened?"

"I caught a fish yesterday, and he was hurt. Daphne threw him back in the lake, and I got mad." Heat simmered in her voice. "She wouldn't listen. He needed to see the vet. I sneaked out of the tent to find him." As fast as her burst of anger came, it vanished, leaving her small and shivering. "I was walking around the edge of the lake. I was trying to find the fish when I heard it." A shudder wracked her. "The horse was crying. Not like a person but... I wanted to help him, so I waded out in the water. He turned and kept going deeper and deeper, and I knew Daphne would be so mad at me, but I followed him. I touched him. Right beside his tail." Her eyes went liquid. "I couldn't get loose. I tried, but I was stuck. I was so scared my bubble just… And then he dragged me under the water."

Her breathing grew faster as she recalled how terrifying that experience had been. I didn't press her for a timeline. When the kelpie hauled her out to parade her around didn't matter now. Only the whys did, and she wouldn't know those.

The air around her distorted, and I pressed her harder while a crack formed in her defenses. "Can you tell me what happened tonight?"

"He was mad. *So* mad." She blinked and shed tears. "The merlady found where we were hiding. She attacked him with a knife." Roni reached under Harlow and produced the slim dagger with a shell-encrusted handle she had tucked into her neoprene top. "This knife." She gulped hard, shut her eyes and lifted her arm. "S-s-she did this."

My gaze zeroed in on her elbow, slid down her forearm, and I braced myself for a weeping stump that ended at her fragile wrist, a brutal amputation to match the other victims, but Roni's hand was whole. More than whole, a cut of raw meat stuck to her palm where Harlow had sliced her free of the kelpie.

I swallowed hard and tasted acid in the back of my throat.

"The horse—he had a tail like hers—like a fin. He hit her in the head with it, and it cut her throat. She couldn't breathe, so I made her a bubble like mine. Then we hid in a tunnel the horse couldn't fit into until he went away. I waited for a long time before..." Her gaze dropped to Harlow sprawled limp across her lap. "She was bleeding so much...and then it stopped."

The faint rise and fall of Harlow's chest gave me the strength to keep calm. She had survived the ordeal, and medicinal magic could work miracles...if we got her to a medic quickly. Roni might not be ready to trust me yet, but Harlow was human. She had healing charms, but those were patches, not fixes. I had to nudge the girl again and hope having someone to talk to calmed her enough she could relax the tension coating the surface of her bubble.

One of Harlow's gills must have been damaged when the kelpie attacked, but I didn't see any signs of the wound. Trapped between inhaling oxygen like a human and filtering air from the water like a fish, it was a miracle she had lasted this long. The other gill needed to be removed, and gods only knew how to do that without cutting into her. Until it was gone, I doubted her lungs would fill and function properly. I had to act now. Either the wall came down or I hunted down the Garzas and paid them whatever it took to burst her bubble.

"You were brave. So brave. You saved Harlow's life." I kept my tone even as I praised her. "But I have to ask you to be brave one more time. I need you to take a deep breath, focus on your magic, and lower the bubble so I can get her the help she needs. Can you do that?"

"I can t-t-try." Her eyes shut, and the air pulsed. A tendril of Harlow's hair fell through and tickled the sand beneath her. "Hurry. I can't hold it much longer."

Careful not to spook Roni with sudden movements, I shifted Harlow toward me and hooked my hands under her arms. I dragged until her heels left furrows in the sand. I checked her pulse—steady but weak—and examined the jagged edges of the wound that had fused together into an angry red chevron pattern zigzagging from her collarbone to her jawline, bisecting one of the artificial gills. With one functioning gill and the use of Roni's air bubble, I was betting the culprit here was blood loss. Harlow must have used one of the emergency healing charms on herself.

"Here." Roni extended the blade toward me. "It's pretty. She might want it back."

Our fingers brushed when I grasped the handle, and her magic tingled up my arm. *Sylph.* I should have remembered that sooner. Her magic must have allowed her to filter oxygen through the film of her protective bubble. "I'll make sure she gets it." I tucked the dagger into my belt. "Do you want me to help you out now? Or do you want to wait for your mom?"

Magic shimmered around her, and iridescent rainbows slid over the bubble's hull as it solidified. "It won't let go." She tucked the hand clotted with kelpie flesh by her leg, out of sight. "I'll stay." Roni shifted positions, drawing her knees up to her chest and wrapping her free arm around them. Her forehead lowered, bracing on her kneecaps. "It's safer in here anyway."

A warm hand landed on my shoulder. *Graeson.* No wonder she had withdrawn from me. The sight of him naked wasn't doing the already traumatized girl any favors.

His fingers tightened. "We have to leave."

Car doors slammed nearby, and I made my choice. "I can't abandon them."

"Ellis…" A frustrated growl entered his voice.

"Graeson, I said no." I twisted to stare up at him. "You should go before they catch you."

His scarred hands lifted a damp lock of my hair. "May I?"

Really? He wanted to smell me at a time like this? Was it some kind of shifter-style farewell? "Suuurrre," I drew out the word.

Faster than a blink, he willed his index finger to lengthen, its claw to elongate, and he sliced through the clump above his fist, leaving him with a six-inch hank of my hair. The control it had taken for such a precise shift must have been incredible. I smoothed a hand down the cut length.

"Be careful." He clutched his prize, color high in his cheeks, and my stomach fluttered. "See you soon."

Before I found the correct response to getting an impromptu haircut via a warg claw, he was gone. Not a single golden eye winked in the darkness. The pack had fled.

Worrying the shorn ends between my fingers, I sank down next to Harlow, wincing when the sharp edges of her dagger's handle dug into my side. Shifting to one hip, I withdrew the blade and set it beside her in case she craved the security of a weapon when she roused. She remained still where I laid her, and I pressed two fingers to the underside of her blemished jaw. A weak pulse fluttered under her skin, comforting me. I rubbed her arm and made promises I knew I couldn't keep under my breath.

The conclave would be here soon. They could arrange for a transfusion and a burst of magic to boost her recovery. I had to believe they would make it in time.

"Step away from the body and put your hands in the air."

I did as the masculine voice instructed. "I'm Agent Camille Ellis with the Earthen Conclave." I yelled loud enough to be heard from his position. "This is Harlow Bevans. She's a consultant." I linked my fingers in the air over my head. "She's lost a lot of blood. She needs medical attention."

"Medics," the same man boomed. "You've got patients waiting."

Two men carrying a stretcher between them crested the rise and jogged toward me. They shuffled me aside and set to work on Harlow with steady hands and low conversation that comforted me. Each anticipated the other's need, and they worked in tandem to examine her.

A lean man emerged from the trailhead, trundled down to me, grasped my elbow and hauled me in the direction where he first appeared. His eyes were wide set and green, his skin dark. Magic zipped through me at his touch. *Bean sidhe*. Unsettling choice for a search-and-rescue squad volunteer. I hoped the presence of a death portent meant he'd drawn the short straw, not that he carried a message.

"I need to speak with Magistrate Vause." I let him lead me away from the scene marshals were scurrying to secure. A guy with a spotlight tucked under his arm shuffled past. Another carried a flipper I assumed went to his wet suit. A woman walked with her head down as she studied a clipboard, and two more men barked orders into walkie-talkies with a fervor that would have done Graeson proud. "She can vouch for me."

A grim expression pinched his eyes. "I'll have someone higher on the food chain dial her up and see what she has to say."

"Can I wait here while you contact her?" I jerked my chin toward Harlow. "I'd like to keep an eye on my friend."

A frown marred his preternaturally smooth forehead when his gaze eased past my shoulder.

"What is it?" Heart in my throat, I whipped my head toward the lake. At first glance I didn't register a problem. A soft-spoken marshal was engaging Roni while a man in jeans snapped pictures of the kelpie's corpse. A woman decked out in a headlamp documented paw-print impressions as a tall man walked the dock with a phone pressed to his ear. Then my gaze honed in on the twin trenches dug by Harlow's heels where I had dragged her through the sand. The medics were gone. Harlow was too. "Where did they take her?"

"I don't—" He scratched behind his ear. "They must have taken another path and circled back to the ambulance."

I was already shaking my head. The wargs had done heavy recon on the area to prepare us for all eventualities. I was familiar with all possible exits near the dock in case I needed a quick escape route. "There is no second path." Not for a quarter of a mile in the opposite direction, and no way would two guys with a stretcher decide to forge their own trail when there was a perfectly good path right here. "I'm heading down there."

"Wait." A string of foreign swears followed me. "Agent Ellis."

Shrugging off the bean sidhe's warnings, I ran for the cluster of activity. I grabbed the first marshal I saw by his collar. "Where's the mermaid?"

He swatted me aside with a meaty fist. *Ursine shifter*. "Lady, I don't know what you're quacking about."

"There was a mermaid." I pointed to the drag marks in the sand. "Right there."

"Hey, Phil, did you see a mermaid?" he yelled to the guy with a flipper.

"Nope." He waved at me with the webbed hunk of plastic. "I doubt I would have been hauled out of bed at the butt crack of dawn if they already had a mermaid on site. Wasn't there a contractor working these things? Whatever happened to her?"

"Yes." I pointed at my feet. "That was her. She was right here. Ask the bean sidhe. He can tell you I'm not crazy."

"Leonard?" the ursine called. "What's all the noise about?"

"There was a mermaid." A cold spark lit his eyes, and his gaze shot to the forest as if magnetized. "I saw her myself."

"Come on, lady. Think about it." The ursine shifter must have heard my molars grinding. "This close to water? She probably ducked into the lake to heal."

"She's a saltie." Admitting Harlow was human and that's why she wouldn't have returned to the water to regenerate was a bad idea. Harlow was defenseless in her current state. Humans were soft, their bellies tender, and every fae here was a predator. "I'm going to search the woods."

"Don't wander far." Leonard's voice thickened like his mouth had trouble forming the words. "Stay where I can see you. If I have to bring you down, you won't like it."

Chills swept over me. No. I suppose I wouldn't. I'd had enough near-death experiences for one night, thanks. I wasn't about to pit my pitiful athletic abilities against a death-touched fae. Death always won in the end.

The sky lightened. Violet clouds faded to ones with soft pink lining. The brighter conditions made searching easier. Wargs—on two legs and four—had trampled the area. There was no hope of picking a single path as the one medics might have taken. Careful to stay in sight of Leonard, I swept the outskirts of the forest for a hint of where the trio had gone. Several yards deeper than I should have ventured, a dark blob puddled on a smattering of leaves. Casting a wary glance over my shoulder, I located the bean sidhe. His rich skin had paled, and he wet his lips as though a fierce hunger had ignited in him. Making use of his distraction, I stalked deeper into the woods. I toed the clump with my boot, and it made a squishing sound. Confident the mass wasn't something disgusting, I bent down and pinched what I now felt was a ball of wet fabric between my fingers.

Harlow's shorts. Not just any shorts, but the enchanted pair that sprouted scales when exposed to water. Would an injury sustained to the tail be inflicted on her legs? Had the medics removed clothing in order to treat her?

My faith in the medics' competence plummeted. They had discarded a high magic article of clothing at a crime scene. Tossed aside like rubbish when they should have ended up in an evidence locker at the local marshal's office, she would be pissed when she came to without them and her personal effects bag turned up empty. The shorts held sentimental value as well as being critical to her wellbeing as long as she continued her mermaid charade.

Hairs rose along my nape, stinging as they lifted one by one. Magic, cold and eternal, swirled around my ankles and tickled up my legs. I swiped at a tickling sensation on my cheeks, and my fingers came away bloody. A bone-deep wail of grief saturated the night, shaking leaves from the trees and turning my breath to fog.

The bean sidhe sang with all his soul.

Death prowled the woods with me tonight.

Wiping my fingers on my pants, I ventured farther from the chilling melody of Leonard's song. A glimmer of white caught my eye, and I made my way toward it. The closer I came, the louder the bean sidhe's music hammered at my skull. I stumbled and caught myself against a tree. When my brain translated what I was seeing, my knees buckled and hit the damp earth. The stretcher rested inches away from my ankle, its canvas center torn to shreds. The medics, what was left of them, were scattered in chunks of glistening meat in a six-foot radius.

The speck of white that had caught my eye was Harlow's shell-handled dagger, and it was no longer pristine. The grooves were stained pink, the hilt imprinted with a smudged handprint a size smaller than mine, and the blade glistened crimson.

"Harlow," I cried out, voice ragged, her shorts squelching in my grip. "*Harlow.*"

The static thrum of white noise answered me. My ears ached, and my throat itched where thin rivulets of blood dried and cracked.

A fly buzzed my nose, and I swatted it aside. Fingers shaking, I reached out and touched a fractured elbow. *Dola.* This medic had been one of the Slavic spirits who embodied human fate. I wondered if he had foreseen this end. Numbed by the shock, I sent my magic probing, and there it was, as I had known deep in my bones it would be. That now-familiar sheen of energy that coated everything Charybdis touched with his magic permeated the corpse.

The ounce of relief I experienced at the kelpie's death evaporated. Separating the Charybdis persona from the kelpie had been a struggle as I battled doubts over what manner of creature or creatures had pitted themselves against us. Kneeling here, I resonated all the certainty I previously lacked.

This was incontrovertible proof. Charybdis was a separate entity, and he was still very much alive.

I stood and skirted the dead medics, walked into the underbrush and called out to Harlow. Charybdis, being a creature of Faerie, would have understood the bean sidhe's wail and fled. My cries failed to illicit a response from Harlow, but it summoned the others, who, after restraining me with a Word, resumed the search.

Jaw flexing with the force of keeping my mouth shut, I stood there like a model prisoner. Arguing would slow down the hunt, and my pride wasn't worth so much that I couldn't model steel bracelets for a few minutes until the paranoia of finding me standing alone by yet another corpse, two in fact, died down.

The kelpie was the first strike and these two the second and third. As far as they were concerned, until Vause verified my credentials, I was out.

Harlow's disappearance had failed to sway the marshals—the prejudice against mermaids ran deeper than I ever imagined in the waterfront towns where Charybdis had chosen to strike—but two of their own had been slaughtered, and that lit a fire under them.

"That Ellis?" A squat man with a rolling gait snuffled in my direction. "Magistrate Vause is asking for her."

"I would take the call," I said, wiggling my fingers, "but I'm tied up at the moment."

"Lady, she wants a face-to-face." He snorted loudly through his nose with an open mouth. "I've got orders to escort you to the safe house in Falco."

"We can handle things here," Leonard assured me as he approached. "You've done your job. Now let us do ours." A sparkle made his eyes dance, and his cheeks were flush. Death looked good on him. "We'll locate the one responsible."

"Find the mermaid." I made it an order. "She's a victim here too."

Good old Leo sighed his counter-Word and unbound my hands. "I'll be in touch."

I wouldn't hold my breath.

Under the watchful eye of my new escort, I made my way down to the original crime scene, which still buzzed with activity as marshals attempted to coax Roni from her bubble. After the bean sidhe's performance, I could have told them that shield between her and the rest of the fae world wasn't going anywhere.

I broke away from my escort and darted toward the pier before his meaty fist closed over my upper arm. "Give me a minute."

"Hold up." He fell behind after a few steps, panting hard as his thick body protested the vigorous exercise. "I didn't say nothing…about making no pit stop."

"Be right back," I called over my shoulder, scooping up a broken tree limb on my way to the pier.

"Make it…quick." One long wheeze dissolved into a coughing fit. "Be grateful…I'm a nice…guy."

I was grateful all right. That he was too out of shape to catch me.

My knees trembled as my feet thumped over the warped planks. My stomach soured when I pressed it against the wood, inhaling rot and dampness, getting as close to the rippling water as I dared. Using the stick, I pried the barnacle from the leg of the pier and hauled it up beside me. As the material repelled the last of the moisture, the crusted, pasty exterior darkened to brown leather. I opened it, shoved the balled-up pair of shorts inside the center pouch and hot-footed it back to my escort.

The marshal gathered wind in his barrel chest for an argument, but I slid the bag over my shoulders like I had every right to wear it. “Sorry about that.” I adjusted the tight straps to fit my taller frame. “All my ID is in here. I didn’t want to leave it behind.”

“Dames,” he grunted. “Need anything else, Princess?”

“This is all,” I assured him.

“Hurry up.” He beckoned me to follow. “I ain’t paid enough to play chauffeur. I ought to be out there helping find whoever killed Rogers and Donohue, not carting some fancy-pants agent out to Falco.”

I tuned out his grumbling, and my shoulders tensed as hiccupped bawling erupted. Roni cupped a cellphone to her ear thanks to the persistent marshal who managed to weaken a spot in her shield, and she rocked while crying her eyes out to the person on the other end. The tension drained from me, allowing me to slip back into that comfortably numb space where the last twenty minutes hadn’t happened, where Harlow was safe and Charybdis was defeated, and I resumed picking my way toward the fleet of black SUVs. My stride hitched thinking of the many times Graeson had stuffed me into the backseat of similar vehicles. But there was no warg to twist my arm this time. I climbed inside of my own volition, and let my lids droop closed to keep from checking the forest for the burn of golden eyes.

CHAPTER EIGHTEEN

The stocky fae drove me back to Falco, Alabama with his meaty fists clamped on the wheel and the blare of country music in my ears. His humming reminded me of the scratch of a match striking, but he seemed happy enough now that our trip was underway, and I didn't feel like talking, so I let him play songbird.

We reached the safe house early enough most fast food places were still serving breakfast, but I wasn't hungry. I did help myself to chai from the food service station before allowing him to escort me to a tidy office with a name I wasn't familiar with engraved on a plaque on the door. The woman sitting behind the pressboard desk, however, was someone I knew well.

"Magistrate Vause." I turned the cup in my hands, allowing the hot liquid to warm me through the paper. I told myself it was because my fingers were chilly from the AC and not because I had been evicted from a crime scene. "It's nice to see you again. So soon."

One of her delicate eyebrows winged high on her forehead. "I somehow doubt that."

The marshal rubbed a hand over his bristly hair as though straightening it. He must not have counted on getting this close to the magistrate. Usually a private audience took months and an appointment. Which meant he probably didn't realize she had her guards tucked somewhere nearby. I could almost feel their warm breath tickling my nape.

"You may go." She flicked her fingers toward the marshal, who bowed his head.

"Yes, Magistrate." Flushing bright red, he squealed out her title.

Once the door shut behind us, she withdrew a button-sized charm, placed it on the desktop and crushed it with a black metal stapler. My ears popped as the spell activated. If Vause felt the change in pressure, she gave no outward indication.

"What news do you have from Abbeville? Has Harlow been found?" I seized control of our meeting by asking the first rapid-fire questions. "Have they located Charybdis?"

"Charybdis is dead." She squared her shoulders, preparing for a fight. "I was sent pictures of his corpse for confirmation."

A prickling sensation told me we weren't on the same page. "So they found the person responsible for the medics' deaths?"

"You left the state without checking out of your hotel room." She dusted the used charm into the trash bin. "Where did you go?"

She offered up her palm, and the scent of hand sanitizer perfumed the room as it squirted from thin air. Invisibility? That was a dangerous magic, though it shouldn't surprise me to learn the conclave employed it for their high-profile members.

Two could play this game. "I touched one of the corpses, and I'm ready to swear before the full senate of magistrates that whatever killed those medics gave off the same magical signature present at all the previous crime scenes." I stared her down. "My skills are documented, and my identifications have never been contested."

"You were last seen exiting your hotel and getting into a cab." Her clear gaze never left mine as the two different conversations merged into one. "The warg followed minutes later. Where did you go?"

"You had someone following me?" That tidbit of information shouldn't have surprised me. Then the implications of her statement sank in, and fury trembled in my voice. "What are you insinuating?"

"I have made no insinuations," she informed. "I have stated facts in an attempt to clarify your whereabouts during the past few days. As to your former question, yes. I did not trust the warg, and I assigned a guard to you for your protection."

I held in my snort and almost choked on it. A guard. Assigned for *my* protection. No doubt her plant had texted her updates on our every move. Nice.

"I have other information at my disposal. Either I reconstruct the timeline with possible errors, or you can report to me now." She cocked her head, expecting a recitation of dates and times and other damning intel. "The choice is yours," she prompted, her gaze tagging the chair opposite hers. "Do have a seat. You must be tired from your activities last night."

I sank into the plush cushion and debated how much to confide in the magistrate I wasn't sure I trusted anymore. I chose the safer option, the one where she filled in blanks and I corrected her when she got things wrong. "How much do you know?"

"A substantial amount," she said, not falling for the ploy. "Enough that any deviation will be apparent."

"Graeson met me in my hotel room. He wanted to discuss the case. He asked for my help with a plan he had concocted. I declined." I kept it short and to the point. "He refused to leave my room until I heard him out. I declined that too and left when he refused to go." She nodded encouragement, and I continued. "I noticed Harlow hadn't returned from the Sardis Lake site yet, and I made the decision to go to her, hoping by the time I returned the warg would have lost interest and left. At the site, I was unable to locate Harlow. Graeson appeared, without invitation, and we searched for her together."

"Did you feel threatened by the warg?" she interjected.

"No." There was no hesitation in my answer. "He would never hurt me."

"Hmm," she replied. "You sound certain of that."

A tingle of doubt spread through me. I got the impression I had given away a personal truth I should have kept to myself, but it was too late now. If Vause had been following Graeson and me as closely as she claimed, she would know the warg had formed an attachment and that I was, sadly, not immune to his charms. Graeson was a gorgeous specimen of wargdom. I had seen every inch of him nude, many times, and had yet to isolate a single physical flaw. No. Those emerged as soon as he opened his mouth. The man was a master manipulator.

"The Fury, Letitia Rebec, captured us," I continued, to stall her next segue. "I was knocked unconscious and—"

"I'm aware of those proceedings." Vause waved a thin hand, appearing eager to reach a specific point in my narrative. "I have an eyewitness account of every moment from the time you left the hotel to the time you were taken into custody by Mr. Graeson and his associate, Adele Preston." She leaned forward. "You were missing for several days, unwilling or unable to return any of my phone calls, and the next I hear of you is through a liaison informing me that you were in Abbeville and asking for me. What brought you to Abbeville, Camille? How did you end up in the middle of a crime scene?"

I told her the truth. "Graeson believed that area was the next location where the kelpie would strike."

"How did he come across this information?"

"He gave a scale we found at the Brushy Creek site to—" despite my irritation with them, I covered for the Garzas anyway, "—a witch. He used it to power a divination spell."

"Interesting. Not many packs employ witches." Her gaze sharpened. "What else did this witch divine?"

"All I know is what Graeson told me." I spread my hands in a helpless gesture. "He claimed the kelpie would take its next victim in Abbeville, Mississippi, and that's why he brought me there."

That Charybdis had been predicted to make an appearance in Tennessee, I kept to myself, unsure whether that timeline had been negated by the kelpie's death.

"What did he hope you would accomplish that his own people could not? He didn't allow you access to any resources, which means your conclave contacts would have proven useless." When I didn't immediately answer, she gave a knowing nod and her lips thinned. I glimpsed the tip of an emotion too vast to be labeled as anger there, but she blinked, and her mask slid back into place. "I see. I suspected that might be the case."

Angry he beat you to the punch? The words almost flew out of my mouth, but I clamped my jaw shut and caged them. Pissing off a magistrate was far more dangerous than yanking Graeson's tail ever could be.

"Wargs are practical beasts. Graeson saw Lori, and he began plotting a way to use her." Vause rubbed a finger over the creased skin between her eyebrows. "That was my fault. I acted…rashly…in allowing him to sit in on the McKenna girl's interview. I apologize for sharing your secrets with him so openly."

"I would have agreed to help if he'd asked." The urge to defend Graeson loosened my jaw. "I could have escaped if I'd wanted to." I amended that to, "He would have released me if I'd asked."

Her hand dropped, and she stared at me. "Why didn't you?"

"I felt he had information pertinent to the case." I shifted in my chair under the weight of her consideration. "Since native species are hesitant to trust fae, it seemed like a good opportunity to learn what they knew."

Vause let that statement hang suspended between us. "Yet you made no attempt to share this information with the conclave."

"He took my phone." For the first time, I was glad for it. "Wargs don't need them for interpack communication. None of the wargs I saw carried one. As isolated as we were, I doubt I would have had reception in any case, so the point is moot."

Not a total lie. I had held Daphne's phone in hand, but I hadn't checked the bars for signal strength. As far as I knew, I was telling her the truth.

"You aren't on trial here, Camille," Vause soothed. "Despite his methods, I can't argue with the results. The two of you managed to do what we could not. You brought down Charybdis and saved a girl's life." Her voice remained cool. "If you are satisfied with your treatment, then we won't press charges against Mr. Graeson or the Chandler pack."

"I appreciate your generous offer, and I accept. I am satisfied on that front." I mounted my next argument. "But the kelpie was not Charybdis. The evidence supports magical tampering with the crime scenes, as well as the odd behavior of the beast itself. I posit that Charybdis is a separate entity. We killed a vassal, a thrall, something, but the man behind the murders is still free and killed two more fae today, long after the kelpie's witnessed time of death."

"A full investigation is underway," she assured me.

"What about Harlow?" I still had no answers. "Have they found her?"

"The changeling has not been located, no."

My spine went stiff at the mention of Harlow's heritage.

"I see you were aware of the circumstances of the girl's birth. For your sake I hope that is a recent development." Her lips formed a moue of disappointment. "After Wink—" ice formed on her next words, "—we couldn't afford to be ignorant of her deficits. We had her tested and her background thoroughly researched beyond the superficial probing she and other minor contractors receive."

"What Harlow is—or isn't—doesn't concern me. It doesn't change to fact she's one of ours, and she deserves our help." I scooted to the edge of my seat. "I would like to return to Abbeville and provide support for the team."

"That's not possible." Vause lifted a pen and then discarded it. "Your involvement with the warg has been called into question. Your defense of him, of his actions, even now, is too impassioned to believe you're ambivalent toward him. Even if I could defend you against those accusations, you were close to Harlow. You can't be circumspect." She softened her voice. "Given your past history, it was foolish of me to recruit you for this case."

Bitterness coiled in my chest. "You're taking Charybdis from me."

"Go home. Rest. You've been granted two weeks of leave time. Paid, of course." She stood and smoothed imagined wrinkles from her skirt. "I will forward any updates on your friend that I receive."

Two weeks. The pronouncement hit me with the force of a backhand. Paid or not, being shut out hurt. Aunt Dot would be thrilled about the forced vacation, but the idea of sitting at home that long made my skin itch. Foolish or not, Vause had recruited me to unmask Charybdis, and after witnessing his carnage, I had no intentions of leaving his capture up to the conclave. Maybe I would take Graeson up on his offer of cooperation after all.

Vause waited until my hand was on the doorknob and my back was to her before extending an olive branch. "A few months ago a death goddess, the Morrigan, attempted to escape Faerie and take up residence in the mortal realm."

A zing shot down my spine. *The Morrigan*. That was the name Thierry had danced around in Wink. I had summoned the goddess once, back when I was still a marshal. The Morrigan had access to the mortal realm. Why press to make residence here permanent when she had the best of both worlds? I hesitated, waiting to see if Vause enlightened me.

"Some believe she encouraged the cutting of the tethers connecting this realm with the fae realm in order to prevent extradition." Vause turned introspective. "You might ask yourself what a death goddess fears enough to jump realms and burn the bridges after her. You might also ask yourself who offered her the match."

"The boy's death in Wink wasn't related to Charybdis." I slowly faced Vause. "You knew that before you sent me to Texas, didn't you?" I leaned back against the door. "You wanted me to know about the portal." Another thought occurred to me. "You wanted me to meet Thierry."

"The kraken had to be dealt with sooner or later." A speck of a smile teased her lips. "I chose sooner."

"Why not tell me that outright? I could have flown out and grabbed a cup of coffee with her without all the pretense." I squeezed the knob until it squeaked. "A good man might not be dead—his wife incarcerated and his children parentless—if I hadn't intervened."

"It was necessary for you to visit Wink in more ways than one." Her mood darkened. "There were restrictions placed on me meant to curb my involvement. A few of the more cumbersome vows had to be lifted before this conversation could occur."

"You mean the blood oath I pledged to Thierry." I thumped my head against the flat of the door. "Did you bribe her to initiate me?"

Our chat, the baring of our souls, couldn't have been scripted, right? Who was I kidding? Vause lived to dig deep into the tender heart of people to discover what weaknesses she might use against them.

"No." She laughed, actually laughed, out loud. As startled as she was, I had to wonder when the last time was that something had tickled her funny bone. I knew the feeling. Coaxing laughter out of the reserved subset we belonged to tended to require herculean effort few made. "Thierry would do the opposite of what I asked to spite me. She believes in the conclave as an institution, but she has no love for magistrates."

Unexpected relief spiraled through me. I liked the no-nonsense marshal, and I fully intended to make good on her offer to dial her up if I needed help. Due to my current circumstances, I had to hope her rebellious spirit lent itself to helping out those of us about to lose access to restricted information, including sending me a copy of the portal breach video.

Another pressure wave popped my ears. While I was vacillating, Vause had killed the privacy spell.

"An escort has been arranged to bring you to the airport." Vause held her hands clasped in front of her. "Your belongings were retrieved from Abbeville, and your flight home has already been booked."

I accepted our meeting was over. "If you hear anything about Harlow…"

"You will be the first person I contact," she assured me.

I exited her borrowed office and dumped the chai I hadn't touched in the trash. It didn't hit me until then that my lips had tingled more than once since Thierry bound me when I spoke to Vause. The magistrate knew so much…and yet… I must hold a piece of the puzzle she had yet to learn. There was only one thing for it. I had to speak to Thierry again.

I located the fae who had escorted me to Vause's dressing down. "I'm ready to go."

The man shoved onto his feet with a donut clenched between his teeth and a cup of coffee wrapped in one fist. He set off toward the parking lot, and I trailed him. Music on the ride to the airport was as twangy as the soundtrack to Falco had been. He pulled next to the curb and popped the hatch. I took the hint, climbed out with Harlow's bag tucked under my arm and grabbed my carry-on from the trunk. The second the latch caught, the SUV's tires spun, burning rubber toward Abbeville.

Rooting through the pockets of my overnight bag, I touched a slice of heavy plastic. My cell? I hadn't spotted it since I woke at the Rebec home. I powered it up as I strolled through the lobby of the airport and checked my messages. My thumb was hovering over the first digit of Aunt Dot's number when the screen went dark.

"Dead battery," I grumbled. "Perfect."

In the age of cellular supremacy, phone booths were long extinct. I had no idea if my charger had survived Graeson's and then the conclave's packing efforts, and I was too tired to dig through my belongings to figure it out. That meant waiting in line at the customer service kiosk, which was slightly less painful than visiting a dentist when in a major airport. I blessed this bucolic Alabama town as I walked right up to the counter.

"My battery died." I pasted on a smile that didn't come close to matching the brunette behind the counter's megawatt grin and dropped the bags at my feet. "Do you have somewhere I can make a call?"

"Sure, hon." The attendant set a light blue phone with a dark blue cord on the edge of her desk. "Instructions for dialing out are printed on the handset."

"Great." I dialed Aunt Dot, my fingers foreign on the raised square buttons. "I appreciate it."

"No problem." She stepped away and gave me a modicum of privacy.

"Pumpkin," Aunt Dot boomed in my ear. "Did you get my message?"

"No. Sorry. My phone died." The sound of her voice was a balm to my nerves after the last twenty-four hours. "I just wanted to call and let you know I'm at the airport. I should be home in time for dinner."

"Home?" She cackled merrily. "Honey, have you spoken to Cord lately?"

"Yes. Wait— What?" My heart shriveled to the size of a raisin. "How do you know Graeson?"

"He called first thing this morning and explained *everything*." She sounded peppier than she had in months. "He told me how you met and fell in love working a case together. He sounds like a doll. He's so smitten with you, it's precious. I can't believe you didn't mention him to me. How tall is he? Does he have a lot of muscles? He sounds gorgeous. Do you have a picture you can email Isaac? No. Don't do that. I'll wait. I want to be surprised."

Me? In love with Cord Graeson? "How did he get your number?" I answered my own question. "He copied my contacts while he had possession of my phone." Her indulgent laughter didn't help my mood. "What do you mean you'll wait? Wait for what?"

"You really don't know?" She clucked her tongue with budding fondness. "That boy promised he would clear things up with you."

"Things? What things?" My shrill voice kept rising. "What are you talking about?"

"Cord said you two are getting close, and he wants to meet the family before things get serious." A sigh blasted my ear. Clearly, I was ruining her fun. "He owns acreage in Georgia. Did you know that? He invited the whole family to drive down so we could spend the week getting to know each other."

My fingers clenched around the phone until the plastic shell creaked. Vause must not be the only one keeping tabs on me. What would Graeson have done if Vause hadn't suspended me? *I don't want to know.* I was learning he was a warg with a plan for every possible contingency and that he had no qualms taking what—or who—he wanted. The thing was, with Charybdis still at large and my ties to the conclave temporarily severed, I didn't mind the idea of having backup when it came to protecting my family. Getting Aunt Dot and my cousins out of Tennessee until Charybdis reared his head again relaxed the part of me that had been fretting over the killer's apparent fascination with my current home state.

Had Graeson mentioned this plan, I might not have laughed in his face. Now we would never know, because he did what he always did, which was hatch a scheme, assume his way was best, and expect everyone else to fall in line behind his hairy beta warg ass.

"You don't sound thrilled." A horn blasted in the background, and Aunt Dot swore revenge against the driver of a red Jetta, telling me the caravan was on the move. "It's not too late. Should we pass on his invitation?"

"No." I massaged my forehead. "I just didn't expect Graeson to tell you about us." I clenched my teeth. "He must have wanted to surprise me." Shock was a good word for it. I'd had no idea there was an *us*. Let alone that we had gotten so serious as to involve our families in our relationship. "I have to exchange my ticket, but I'll get there as soon as I can."

Accepting Graeson's hospitality felt a whole lot like strolling into a wolf's den while modeling a Kobe beef necklace, and I knew beyond a shadow of a doubt who would be waiting to collect me at the other end of the flight with warm hazel eyes and a smug grin.

Cord Graeson. Wolf with a taste for vengeance. Man with an agenda. And, apparently, my new boyfriend.

Also by Hailey Edwards

Araneae Nation

A Heart of Ice #.5
A Hint of Frost #1
A Feast of Souls #2
A Cast of Shadows #2.5
A Time of Dying #3
A Kiss of Venom #3.5
A Breath of Winter #4
A Veil of Secrets #5

Daughters of Askara

Everlong #1
Evermine #2
Eversworn #3

Black Dog

Dog with a Bone #1
Dog Days of Summer #1.5
Heir of the Dog #2
Lie Down with Dogs #3
Old Dog, New Tricks #4
Stone-Cold Fox

Gemini – Black Dog Series

Dead in the Water
Head Above Water

Wicked Kin

Soul Weaver #1

ABOUT THE AUTHOR

A cupcake enthusiast and funky sock lover possessed of an overactive imagination, Hailey lives in Alabama with her handcuff-carrying hubby, her fluty-tooting daughter and their herd of dachshunds.

Made in the USA
San Bernardino, CA
11 December 2016